BRADEN QUINLAN

THE ERRORUNSIN

Contents

Acknowledgement

Thank you, Mom and Dad for your continued support and encouragement. Thank you also to Parker for again providing feedback to make my second book even better.

1

The Sentinels

The Edhrine stood in a command center, wearing iron armor and a helmet with a small visor. Inside the visor was a black cloth he could see out through, but none could see in through. He studied a map with several of his officers, who also wore iron armor but with their faces visible.

One of his officers, named Tim, spoke, "We should move in the troops on this flank. It will distract the Sentinels, so we can advance the troops here on their flank."

"Do so," the Edhrine agreed. He looked out the window of the small fort, surveying the battle before him. The Sentinels executed a bold move. They sent a few soldiers from their main army to occupy a thin strip of land on the Edhrine's side. It was a foolish tactic that reminded him of the time when the Sentinels attacked him unprovoked, a few years before this battle. During that previous assault, they invaded a small village while attempting to seize the minerals within. This attack did not make the Edhrine happy, but it was a minor attack on a minor outpost by a minor faction, and nobody died. Because nobody died, the Edhrine was not bothered. However, the next attack was very deadly. The Sentinels struck a fortified position and killed seventy of the Edhrine's men. At that point, the Edhrine was done playing nice. They were a threat to his nation, and his nation would be in danger until they were defeated. In response to the attack, he swiftly raided their small territory, causing the Sentinels to lose control of several tactical positions and retreat to another area where they had forts. When the Edhrine came to that area, they retreated yet again. Now, the Sentinels held position in the area just north of a mountain range, the Edhormond Mountains, and the Edhrine planned to annihilate them. The Sentinels would surrender or die, and no longer be considered any kind of nation.

"Sir," said a soldier, interrupting the Edhrine's thoughts.

"Yes?" the Edhrine replied.

"The enemy strike force has been defeated. We cornered them and prevented them from escaping back to their forces. We captured them alive."

"I will go talk to them. Soldier, tell the troops on the northern flank to advance in an all-out assault on the Sentinels. We will reinforce them with catapults. Destroy the forts, on top of them if you must. I don't want them returning and fortifying."

"Understood, sir."

After giving orders to the soldier, the Edhrine departed the command center for the prison, followed by two bodyguards. The people he recruited were loyal to him, trusting in his tactical ability and unsurpassed swordsmanship to protect them. He always protected them, defeating any and all attackers. After all, he was an Errorunsin, an ancient, powerful being who was no stranger to war. He was the only one with a nation of humans. The other three Errorunsai, the Mokror, Marantaur, and the Ifloract, were busy raising armies with sorcery. The Edhrine was proficient with sorcery, but he was more interested in conventional armies. By recruiting humans, he prevented potential enemies from recruiting them.

The Edhrine arrived at the prison, which was located in the bottom floor of the fort. He never understood the Sentinel forts. The forts had many design flaws, including the prison being at ground level. In his view, it provided an easy way for prisoners to escape. However, he did not have a fort of his own, so the vulnerable Sentinel fort would have to do. Arriving at his destination, the Edhrine opened the outer door of the prison. He walked into the circular room with several cells built into the wall. Even if the prison was on the ground floor, it possessed an effective layout. If the prisoners escaped their cells, they were still locked in by the much stronger door that secured the entire room.

After surveying the security, the Edhrine scanned the prisoners. They sat in the cells, wearing the clothes they had worn under their armor. "Hello, there," the Edhrine greeted.

A prisoner grumbled.

The Edhrine continued, "I would like to ask you some… questions."

"Really?" the same prisoner said, clearly not surprised.

"Yes, starting with this one. Where is the escape route for your troops?"

"What do you mean?" asked the prisoner, pretending to be confused.

"You know what I mean. Every single time we take over your area, you retreat to another area riddled with your forts. We know you have a way to escape to another area that we probably already kicked you out from years ago. We follow you and you just run in circles. We would like to…end this."

"It's confidential," the prisoner replied, sarcastically.

"Now that you have confirmed you know it, we are not wasting our time asking you. Is this also true of your friends?"

"No. I am the division commander, and the only person in my division that knows. Normally, there would be others, but your men slaughtered everyone but me and a few random soldiers who happened to be in the command center."

"Okay, so we could send those men into the wilderness. Guards."

The Edhrine's bodyguards tensed as a soldier opened the cell of every prisoner except that of the division commander. A few minutes later, the soldiers returned to the prison and announced that they released all prisoners into the wild.

The division commander chuckled.

"What is so funny?" the Edhrine asked.

"You just sent the real division commander into the wild, and he will regroup with our forces who were waiting for him with supplies. Then, they will return to the Sentinels and there is nothing you can do about it. However, he may have left a small surprise with me.

"I am not easily surprised," the Edhrine replied. "I believe the forces that your commander expects to regroup with have been destroyed. Additionally, we did not release the others to the wild. Rather, we transferred them to another prison room. It was too obvious when you sent the division to us. It was a trap, which was also why we removed the gunpowder that you placed along the fort as you were being marched to this cell, in which you will be locked forever."

"I doubt that," the prisoner snapped.

The Edhrine continued, "You may doubt it less than you say. The real division commander was quite impressed that we uncovered his scheme. He told us of the secret exit in exchange for his freedom. When we move out to intercept the rest of the Sentinels, we will let him go, but you and the rest of the men will remain locked in the prisons with enough food and water to survive for only a short time. I hope your forces rescue you before you die."

The prisoner responded, "Whether or not you will defeat us, you will fall as an old nation once did. Another nation attacked them. They were so focused on the attackers that a few small, yet devastating attacks from an entirely different nation defeated them."

"Yes, I am sure we will," the Edhrine snickered. "Should I mention that we captured you today by distracting you with our forces? It is quite similar to your suggestion of our fate."

With that, the Edhrine and his guards left, throwing the food sacks into the middle of the room and opening the man's cell to grant him access to the prison room. They moved the rest of the prisoners with him and closed the gate to the area.

"I hope this works," one of the Edhrine's bodyguards said.

"It will. I highly doubt any aid will come to them. They will die, and pay in part for the attacks," the Edhrine predicted. "Just as the rest of the Sentinels will die, and they will die completely. Nothing will threaten us again once the Sentinels are destroyed. We will finally be safe."

After the Edhrine's army packed up, the Edhrine led his army to the concealed dock where the Sentinels would attempt to leave. Even the Edhrine had to admit that the dock was hidden quite well, in an extremely large cove. Several ships were docked there. The Edhrine had a few divisions of men hide in the ships, while others took cover in small supply shacks and crates.

When the Sentinels arrived, nothing looked out of place. The ships were there, the crates were there, and nothing was moved. The Sentinel commander gave orders to his troops, and they entered the supply shacks and ships to load supplies. After a few minutes, the commander sent more men to check on them. None of the men sent into the ships returned. The Sentinel commander panicked. He ordered his main force to surround him. The only problem was that he was too late. The Edhrine's men stormed out of their hiding places and forced the Sentinel commander to surrender. The Edhrine's army commandeered all of the supplies and ships.

"What should we do now, sir?" a soldier asked.

"Tell the troops to load our possessions onto the ships. Move us to the Sorwondian Plain. Let us see what trading we can do in Sorwond. Unfortunately, they are still repairing the damage from the previous, tyrannical king, but there may be items of value there," the Edhrine said.

The Edhrine's troops loaded the supplies and their new captives aboard the ships and embarked upon the journey to Sorwond. The Edhrine took a position in the back of the ship, finding suitable quarters. He turned the Sentinel commander's quarters into a command center and charted a course for Sorwond. With the supplies from the cove, the Edhrine was nearly guaranteed to get his hands on some valuables and use those valuables to hire more soldiers for their army.

2

The Ambush

The Edhrine was sharpening his longsword to occupy his spare time, when a soldier entered his quarters and spoke, "Sir, you should come see this."

When the Edhrine reached the command center, he was not happy. The wind altered their course and pushed them to the south. Nobody noticed because it happened overnight. They did not realize they drifted nearly twenty miles off course until it was too late.

The Edhrine directed, "Just go to the shore here. It's close to the Sacred River. We can get water from it to avoid using supplies. We can try to make the journey from there."

"Yes, sir," a soldier acknowledged.

Once they reached the shore, the Edhrine watched as his men unloaded supplies. He had a strange feeling of uneasiness. "Men, can you work any faster? I feel that we are not safe here."

One of the soldiers replied, "We are trying, sir. Some of the cargo is heavy."

The Edhrine quickly countered, "Just forget about it. Take what we can carry and get out of here."

Unfortunately, it was already too late. A large force of strange soldiers arrived. The soldiers moved very robotically, in a perfect line. From another direction, another massive force approached. The Edhrine recognized the second force as the Sentinels. The two armies did not appear to be working together. Based on the terrain, they likely couldn't see each other. There was no way to get them to fight one another, which meant that the Edhrine would have to handle both. He was in a bad position. Some of his men were with the ships, still unloading supplies. A few more were tired from the work and were resting on the beach, unaware of the enemy presence.

"Defensive formation! They are coming from the north and east!" the Edhrine shouted.

The available soldiers scrambled to form lines to meet the enemies, but they were too late. The unidentified enemies had archers, and good ones, too. They killed some of the men who were resting. The Sentinels approached in small and tight lines. The Edhrine's archers were busy fighting with the unidentified enemy.

The combined force was killing the Edhrine's troops. The Edhrine himself was dueling the Sentinels, scoring kills. However, the Sentinels who were dueling his men fared well. The Edhrine was losing men fast, and he would be defeated if he did not do something fast.

The Edhrine decided to strategize. He ordered the archers to handle the Sentinels while he fought the unknown enemy. Their archers were getting annoying, but now fewer of his men were dying. Within seconds, for an unknown reason, the unknowns left, allowing the Edhrine to confront the Sentinels with the remainder of his force. He forced the Sentinels to retreat, but not before they rescued their leader from captivity.

The leader had just been unloaded when they came, and was waiting outside the ship with only four of the Edhrine's soldiers guarding him.

The Edhrine called everybody who remained to come in front of the ships. He had lost half of his soldiers. Without his large army, all hopes of destroying the Sentinels faded. He would be lucky if the Sentinels didn't defeat him.

The Edhrine pondered the situation. Without a large force, he could either train his soldiers until they were elite or put up with being a minuscule nation. The Edhrine settled with the former. "Soldiers, we are going to make the journey to Mohraight. We cannot remain here."

A soldier panicked, "They are going to attack us! We're going to be raided! We can't make the journey."

"The unknowns are going to raid us at sea. We don't stand a chance. I'm getting out of this army at Sorwond!" another frightened soldier shouted.

Yet another soldier cried out, "We should stop at Sorwond! We don't want to die fighting for you. You told us you would protect us, and now half of us are dead!"

The Edhrine knew that only a fraction of his forces still remained loyal to him.

"How about this?" the Edhrine announced. "You take a ship to Sorwond, with enough supplies to survive the journey. I will take the two other ships with the men who are still loyal and go to Mohraight for training. You traitorous cowards can go."

With that, the two groups parted ways. The Edhrine and his half-division boarded two of the ships while the traitors loaded supplies and set sail for Sorwond.

The Edhrine went to his quarters. He had half of a division remaining. He started with six divisions. Over the course of the war, he lost two. However, he just lost three and a half in a single day. With only half a division, there was little the Edhrine could do other than get some training with the Mohraight. He knew that they could train his men to be better than the average soldier, but that still would not do. They did not tell all of their secrets to outsiders. If he really wanted elite soldiers, he would need to search further, but Mohraight was his best option right now.

"Set sail for Mohraight," the Edhrine directed, "and ensure someone stays awake to make sure we don't go off course again. We all know what happened last time that happened."

When the Edhrine arrived in Mohraight, he and his men disguised themselves as citizens. They made their way to a mercenary training ground and signed up. They planned to live on the ships that they captured from the Sentinels.

After months of training, the Edhrine moved his forces to other nations in the area. They went to Nacreato for advanced training, sneaking in to avoid suspicion, as the nations of Mohraight and Nacreato were not exactly friends.

After training with Nacreato, they moved throughout the smaller nations, taking the hardest lessons available. The Edhrine's men began to become elites. Nonetheless, the Edhrine knew he could do better. The troops made the journey to Sorwond without being attacked and trained there. Then, they studied the tribal fighting styles of the North Morhor Plain and then the South Morhor Mountains. After that, the Edhrine felt his men were more than thoroughly trained. Now, they just needed better gear. The Edhrine doubted they would win against the elites of other nations with the gear that they had. However, he could not get weapons without drawing attention, so he decided to go to an island… a very specific island.

The Edhrine's men had no clue where they were going, since the Edhrine had only given them a map location. They were not happy to traverse the Mohraight Graveyard. It was the death of many, many ships. The sharp rocks that protruded from the ocean floor were riddled with crashed ships and rotting bodies. Additionally, the destination was not on any maps. Some men thought the Edhrine was going insane. Nevertheless, they eventually reached their destination.

When the men landed, they were more disgusted than before. There were spiders, which were about the same size as a backpack, with black fur. The spiders were eating bodies they pulled in from the Mohraight Graveyard. The Edhrine was completely unaffected by the hideous sights. He calmly led his men to a sewer entrance, which was guarded by spiders. A spider activated a hidden switch that opened the entrance. The Edhrine motioned his men inside, and they reluctantly followed, not wanting to go into a sewer in a spider-infested land.

"What is this place?" a soldier asked.

The Edhrine replied, "This is the home of the Mokror."

"Who is the Mokror?" a different soldier questioned.

The Edhrine explained, "She is another Errorunsin."

"What is an Errorunsin?" the soldiers said in unison.

The Edhrine did not respond. The spiders leading them stopped at a door, and the Edhrine motioned for his men to remain outside as he walked into the room.

"Hello," the Edhrine greeted.

"Hello. How are you?" the Mokror said in return.

"I could be better. I am left with half a division of men. However, they have been training. They only need some gear. Until we can obtain that, I would like to live on the island."

"You could stay in the sewers, but the men won't like that. However, there are ruins of an ancient city that I have never really explored. If you want a base, it would be a good place. You may even find iron. Just don't let anyone trace you to the island."

The Edhrine liked that plan. He exited the room and informed his men that they were moving into some ruins.

"I hope they are nowhere near this sewer system and these spiders," a soldier remarked.

"You will like them, then," the Edhrine told them.

"Good. I've already been here for too long," the soldier replied.

3

The Warship

The Edhrine and his men found the ruined city. The walls were pretty much gone. However, several of the buildings in the center of the ruins remained standing.

"All right. Fan out. Let's see if there's anything left of this civilization that we can use," the Edhrine directed.

After about an hour of searching, they met up back where they started and the soldiers reported in. The men created a map of the ruins they explored.

"There is a forge still standing in this area," a soldier said, gesturing to a point on the map of the city.

"I found some really old iron in this storehouse," said another. "The iron will need to be melted to rid it of any impurities, though. These people did not know how to do that based on the appearance of the iron."

One more soldier reported, "There was a small bar of impure gold in the tower. It may have been valuable then, but with the dirt mixed in, it's probably about as valuable as a rock."

"I wouldn't be so sure. We can melt it down to see how much actual gold it contains," the Edhrine told him. "We can buy some high-quality gear with just a small amount of gold."

"True," the soldier replied and handed the gold to the Edhrine.

Another soldier provided his update, "It looks like they keep their iron in the buildings near the tower that contained the gold. From what I can tell, there used to be a wall around the inner buildings."

After reports from the rest of the half-division, the Edhrine instructed his men to set up camp in the forge. They planned to melt down the iron and gold. Unfortunately for them, there was nothing to burn.

"Sir, we can't find any fuel. There's no wood," a soldier told the Edhrine.

"Let me take care of that," the Edhrine said.

The Edhrine told everyone to leave the forge. They did not know what he planned to do. When they reentered, the fires were lit, although no fuel was visible. The Edhrine had carved fire runes into the furnace walls with an iron dagger. He charged them with sorcery and the bottoms of the furnaces acted like miniature altars. Just as this would make a fire on top of an altar, the Edhrine made a fire in the bottom of the furnace.

"How did you do that?" an amazed soldier asked.

"The Errorunsai are powerful, and I am an Errorunsin. Start melting down the iron and gold."

Weeks later, the entire group was clad in iron armor. It would be difficult to kill them. They also had new weapons specially designed for soldiers with their training. Each had two swords, a spear, a shield, and multiple throwing daggers attached to their gear. They also had a bow and arrows strapped to their backs. It would be very difficult to kill them.

"Men, today we are moving out of these ruins and behind

enemy lines. We are going to locate the Sentinels and infiltrate their forts. Here is the plan. We will surround their command fort and one squad will fire arrows at their men. When the Sentinels approach to kill the squad, two other squads will move in and overwhelm them. The rest will enter the base while the enemy is distracted. Your objective is to find the Sentinel leaders in the area and capture or kill them. I doubt all their leaders are there, but find the ones that are. If it is impossible to get the leaders to the ship, kill them. It is better than those leaders continuing to dispatch forces against us," the Edhrine explained.

"Yes, sir," everyone replied.

"We move out at dawn tomorrow. Load the ships," the Edhrine commanded.

The next day, the Edhrine and his men boarded the ships and began their search for Sentinels. They sailed to the areas where the Sentinels constructed forts, but failed to find them. They did encounter a ship full of Sentinels that tried to attack them. Fortunately for the Edhrine's men, they had elite training. The Edhrine ordered his men to hide in the rooms. The Sentinels scanned the decks and did not find anyone. However, when they attempted to enter the command center, a battle commenced for which the Sentinels were unprepared. The Edhrine's men burst out of hiding and surprised the Sentinels. The Sentinels were pushed back to their own ship, but the Edhrine wasn't satisfied with just defending his ship. He pressed all the way to the enemy ship. Meanwhile, the Edhrine's other ship moved in to block the enemy's escape.

The Sentinels tried to protect themselves from the Edhrine's attack on their ship. They sealed the doors and hid inside, locking the doors with deadbolts. Although the Sentinels were protected, the ship's controls weren't sealed behind doors.

The Edhrine noticed this and declared, "Men, forget trying to get through the doors. Make sure they can't escape their saferooms and then come to the wheel. They are now our prisoners."

The Edhrine's men barricaded the doors of the saferooms and loaded the supplies that they could access onto the Edhrine's ships. Next, they tied the Sentinel ship to one of their own ships and disabled the steering. Now, the prisoners couldn't go anywhere even if they escaped the saferooms. The Edhrine and his men departed the Sentinel ship and returned to their own ships.

They set sail again and spotted another ship approaching. It was much bigger than the Edhrine's ships and armed with catapults. That wasn't good.

"Ramming speed!" the Edhrine shouted. The Edhrine's ships were fitted with a reinforced, pointed bow, and he felt that he may have needed to use that feature.

Luckily for the Edhrine, the ship didn't employ its catapults. Instead, it fired ballistae, which was far less of a threat. The Edhrine's ships approached at ramming speed, but suddenly, the enemy ship fired its catapults at the reinforced bows, inflicting damage to them. Without the reinforced bows, ramming would destroy the ship.

"Retreat," the Edhrine ordered.

As they were leaving, they noticed that the ship had soldiers who wore different armor than the Sentinels. The armor was familiar, though, so the Edhrine figured that it could be an elite unit of Sentinels he had encountered in the past. If the Sentinels possessed more of these ships, he was dead. With a second look, he realized the armor wasn't Sentinel. Rather, it was the armor of the unknowns, the soldiers that reduced him to half of a division.

The Edhrine decided he would first focus on the Sentinels. They attacked him more, and the unknowns would have to wait until the Sentinels were addressed. In any case, a higher priority was the need replace the bows of his ships.

4

The Pursuer

The Edhrine entered the harbor of the capital of Mohraight. Some of his men had gone ahead of him to arrange the purchase of reinforced bows. By the time the Edhrine arrived, the bows were ready to be attached to his ships. Once the bows were affixed to the ships, the Edhrine asked if there were other available upgrades. He had oars installed that could be tucked away, so he could navigate independent of the wind. He also added some ballistae.

The Edhrine thought back to the large warship he had encountered, which belonged to the unknown nation. The unknowns had one large ship, and they might possess more. If so, they could be far graver of a threat than the Sentinels. However, there was no guarantee. Perhaps the Edhrine was unfortunate enough to encounter their most powerful vessel. The Edhrine was more concerned with the Sentinels.

The Edhrine thought about where to go. The Sentinels were evading him and hiding somewhere. He would find out where in time.

As the Edhrine walked towards the harbor at Mohraight, one

of his soldiers approached him. "Sir, we have a visual on the warship that attacked us about a week ago. It's the one that destroyed the bows of our ships."

"Most unexpected," the Edhrine replied. "Disguise our ships as Sentinel ships. Let us hope this unknown nation is friendly with them."

Meanwhile, the admiral of the large ship surveyed the current situation. He knew the enemy ships needed to be repaired. That would mean they would have likely traveled to Mohraight, as it was not far from the clash.

"Sir, we have arrived at Mohraight," an officer reported to the admiral.

"Excellent," the admiral responded.

"Should we send messengers to inform Mohraight of our objective?" the officer asked.

"They will come to us."

Sure enough, several Mohraight ships, with flags bearing symbols resembling upside-down pitchforks, approached the massive warship. None of the Mohraight messengers who boarded the admiral's ship were ever seen again. It wasn't hard to guess what happened.

"Sir, we carried out your orders. We threw the bodies overboard," the officer announced.

Back in the city, the Edhrine inspected his ships. They could pass as Sentinel ships from the exterior. There was no way the enemy would search the inside of every single ship in Mohraight. His men were safe, so long as they wore the Sentinel armor that they had pulled off a few dead enemies. The Edhrine's disguised men walked back and forth on the ship, mimicking the Sentinel practice of guarding the ramp. The men on the other ship were doing the same. The Edhrine never understood why the Sentinels would so obviously march back and forth near the boarding ramp. He preferred for his men to simply stand behind a crate or two and ambush anyone who tried to come and steal loot. The Edhrine watched his disguised men from inside of a closed door. The Edhrine also wore Sentinel armor, but he also had the usual black cloth over his face. If anyone saw the cloth, it would arouse suspicion.

Inside of the massive warship, the admiral looked out the window of the command center. His soldiers crowded the deck of the warship as the warship approached Mohraight. Once at the dock, the ship would drop its ramps and the soldiers would march off to search ships in the harbor. The admiral knew the Edhrine stole Sentinel ships. The admiral also knew that the Edhrine had different armor then the Sentinels. In short, the admiral knew what he was looking for. It was only a matter of time.

From within one of his ships, the Edhrine looked out to sea from the back window of his ship's command center. He decided that he would gain nothing by watching his men pretending to be Sentinels, so he went to observe the enemy warship. It docked at the harbor, and he saw the unknown enemy's soldiers march down the many ramps. The hundreds of soldiers divided into groups of five, with the leader of each group holding a paper. The groups began going through the harbor, reviewing the paper and studying the ships. The Edhrine inferred that the papers were drawings of his ships, and the soldiers compared the ships in the harbor to the drawings. Fortunately, the Edhrine disguised his ships well and his ships resembled Sentinel warships. If the soldiers approached, they would see a Sentinel ship.

Back in the massive warship, the admiral was still looking

out the command center's window when an officer came into the room and interrupted him.

"Sir," announced the officer.

"What?"

"We failed to find the enemy vessel."

"So, you barge in and give me bad news?"

"Uh…"

"Throw this officer overboard."

The admiral resumed looking out the window as two soldiers dragged the officer away. Evidently, the Edhrine had disguised his ships. It was the only way his soldiers could have missed them.

The admiral turned around and directed his attention to his men. "Attention, soldiers. I want you to search all Sentinel ships in the area. If the Sentinels resist…kill them."

Within his ship, the Edhrine peered outside a window. Eleven men, armed with spears and shields, marched toward his ship in an arrowhead formation. They marched in a strange, robotic way. All the soldiers of the unknown empire marched in that way.

"Greet them," the Edhrine whispered. He crouched behind a crate near the men who were pretending to be Sentinels.

When the enemy soldiers came, they did not respond to the greeting. They proceeded to march up the boarding ramp.

"Woah! You don't have permission! Get—," the disguised soldier's protest was interrupted by an enemy soldier's spear going through him.

"Search the ship," the commander of the group directed, calmly pulling his spear out of the dead soldier. The other soldiers walked towards the door of what would be the captain's quarters. The Edhrine rose, silently, from behind the crate.

He drew his iron sword, drawing the attention of the enemy soldiers.

The enemy commander faced the Edhrine and spoke, "Kill him."

The Edhrine dodged three thrown spears coming for him by rolling backward. He jumped over a crate and sent his sword flying into an enemy's head. Dodging another thrown spear, he rolled and retrieved his sword. The Edhrine caught the next javelin and threw it back into the face of the enemy who threw it. Two down, with nine to go.

"Face me!" the enemy commander shouted.

The Edhrine did not need to turn and face him. He sent his sword flying backwards and it hit the commander in the chest. The Edhrine surprised his enemies by rolling forward and punching an enemy rather than retrieving his sword. The punch knocked the enemy's spear out of his hand, and the Edhrine caught it before it reached the ground. That same spear went into its former owner's face. Turning around, the Edhrine hurled it at another soldier. The Edhrine spotted an enemy soldier reaching for his sword. The Edhrine rolled and grabbed the sword just before the soldier could, driving it into the soldier's chest. The other soldiers did not last long fighting against the Edhrine. By the end of the fight, most of the soldiers had their own spears lodged inside of them.

The Edhrine placed the dead bodies in the area in front of his ship. Hopefully, the enemy would assume that robbers or the Mohraight militia ambushed them. The Edhrine was sure to place their spears next to the bodies. Few people used an enemy's own weapon against them, and the Edhrine did not intend to narrow down the possibilities of who may have attacked them.

Infuriated, the admiral stood in his ship's command center. All but two of the group commanders reported back. The admiral sent men to look for the missing commanders, and they found the commanders dead in different places. Evidently, the commanders and their men were ambushed and killed while marching to their destinations. One of the commanders was heading for a Sentinel ship, and the other was going toward the city capitol to force the leaders to surrender. It was very probable that Mohraight militia killed both groups.

The admiral declared, "I want the capitol taken and all of the militia men killed. We do not need the government of Mohraight interfering with this operation."

The Edhrine saw the smoke coming from the capitol of the city. He did not need to guess what the enemy was doing. The Edhrine's maneuver worked. The enemy was fooled into thinking that the Mohraight militia killed those men. Now, the Mohraight government was paying the price. The Edhrine watched the smoke in silence as he heard footsteps approaching behind him.

"Sir," a soldier interrupted, "more enemies are approaching. There are twenty-three of them."

"We can't hide any longer. Send our forces to intercept when they near the ship. We need to depart and continue our war against the Sentinels."

The Edhrine observed as his half-division of men marched down the ramp and stood in a phalanx across from the enemy formation. The two phalanxes stood with about a yard in between them. Nobody made a move, yet.

5

The Raid

"Why do you resist us?" the enemy commander questioned. He was standing behind the phalanx on a large crate. Two bodyguards stood beside him, also on the crate. The phalanx surrounded him, as an ocean surrounds an island.

"Why do you try to kill us?" the Edhrine countered. "Fire!" he shouted. Ballista bolts came from the modified Sentinel ships and tore through the front lines of the enemy phalanx.

"Charge!" the enemy commander ordered.

The Edhrine did not need to order his troops to form a shield wall. They already knew what to do in a battle like this. The Edhrine turned his attention to the enemy commander. The enemy commander remained standing on the crate, now holding a bow. His bodyguards had joined the phalanx. As the enemy commander drew back his bow, he was surprised to find the Edhrine behind him.

The Edhrine put his sword to the commander's neck. "Surrender," he threatened.

The enemy commander ducked down and attempted to punch the Edhrine. He wasn't prepared for the dagger that the

Edhrine had in his other hand. The dagger left the Edhrine's hand and plunged into the commander's side. The Edhrine slipped into the shadows and retreated to his side of the battlefield. The Edhrine was winning. Without a commander, the enemy phalanx was not fighting so well. It was as if they could not think for themselves. Something was not right about these enemies. Their robotic way of marching and their dependence on a commander was not something found in most other armies. It wasn't something found in humans, for that matter.

Once the enemy phalanx was defeated, the Edhrine ordered his men onto the ships. Now, they had to access the Mohraight River. The enemy warship was docked in the harbor, but it could catch up to the Edhrine. The behemoth of a warship had more oars than the Edhrine could count, and likely more oarsmen. That warship would be difficult to outrun.

"Make for the Mohraight Graveyard," the Edhrine commanded.

"I'm sorry, sir, I believe I misunderstood. Could you repeat that order?" a soldier asked, probably thinking nobody was crazy enough to make for the Mohraight Graveyard.

The Edhrine repeated, "Make for the Mohraight Graveyard."

The Edhrine's ships proceeded toward the Mohraight Graveyard. It was hard for any ship to navigate those rocks, let alone a Sentinel warship. However, it would be impossible to navigate the massive enemy warship through them. The warship would need to travel around the Mohraight Graveyard, and that would mean the Edhrine could surprise them by not coming out on the other side.

In the massive warship, the admiral stood in the command center on his ship, watching the Sentinel warships leave.

Sentinel warships were slower than the admiral's ship, so he could catch up. It was, as always, only a matter of time.

The admiral and his warship followed the Sentinel warships. They were catching up when the admiral saw the towering rocks of the Mohraight Graveyard come into view. He also saw the Sentinel ships head straight for them.

"Stop the ship," the admiral directed. "We cannot follow them through the rocks."

"Should we go around?" a Sentinel asked.

"No. Our adversary can exit the graveyard at any point. It is impossible to predict his precise exit point and timing," the admiral explained.

The admiral did not know much about his adversary, save his name, but he did not need to. The emperor told him everything that he needed to know to complete the mission, and he would complete it. He would eliminate the Edhrine at all costs.

Inside the Mohraight Graveyard, the Edhrine marched to the helm of the ship. A soldier there reported that the ship was on course for the next Sentinel target. The Sentinels were reportedly moving their strongholds north of the Edhormond Mountains. The Edhrine proceeded there with his two ships. Sure, the Sentinels had a whole fleet, but they didn't have oars, and they didn't have as many weapons. Using the combined power of the wind and his oars against them, the Edhrine caught up quickly. Soon, he pummeled their ships with ballista bolts, and they tried to flee to the Sentinel forts.

One of the Edhrine's men provided an update, "Sir, one of our ballistae destroyed the window of the captain's quarters on an enemy ship."

"Excellent," the Edhrine replied. "I hope the commander was in there. It will make this battle so much easier for all of us."

The Edhrine watched as the ballistae pummeled the Sentinel ships, hoping to hit a window behind which someone important was hiding. Ballistae were not going to sink the ships, but they could crash through windows or damage anything not inside of the ship.

On the ship whose window had been hit, the Sentinel commander crawled out of the wreckage of his quarters.

"Sir, are you okay?" one of his men asked.

"Yes," replied the commander, as he stood up and surveyed his quarters. A ballista bolt went straight through the window. Shards of broken glass pierced and killed the man that the commander was talking to. The commander was lucky, but he had glass stuck in almost every gap in his armor.

"Alright," the commander began, "we need t—." He was interrupted by a ballista bolt that hit him in the side, sending his body overboard.

The Edhrine steadied the ballista he was aiming. He had decided to do this himself, and he had knocked the enemy commander right off the ship with a carefully aimed shot. He did the same to the shocked man who was standing alongside the enemy commander. The personnel aboard the commander's ship began to panic. The Edhrine managed to position his ship alongside the commander's ship, and the barrage of carefully-aimed ballista bolts sent several Sentinels overboard, one of which was the helmsman. Without a helmsman, the ship was effectively disabled.

"Chase the other ships to the Sentinel forts. Leave this one here," the Edhrine ordered.

The Edhrine's ships turned and forced the Sentinels to either make for the forts or be destroyed by a barrage of ballista bolts. The back of Sentinel ships had barriers that prevented them from taking damage from behind. The Edhrine had strategically positioned his ships. As a result, the only way for the Sentinels to use those barriers was to put their backs to the Edhrine and face the Sentinel forts. From there, they would make the predictable move of going into the forts. The Edhrine knew what he was going to do. He decided to wait. He let the Sentinels move into their forts. After all, the Edhrine had to organize his troops.

When the Sentinels were inside their forts, the Edhrine made sure that there were no ships in their secret escape route. Then, he surrounded the Sentinels. Things were going very well.

Some time later, a Sentinel messenger was sent for the Edhrine for him to begin "negotiating" with the Sentinels. The "negotiations" were really a trap set by the Sentinels. The negotiating table had a few already dead people sitting at it, thanks to the Edhrine. The Edhrine took cover behind a chair as Sentinels pummeled the room with near-endless thrown daggers. The Edhrine gave them some credit. They devised a plot to lure him in, thinking that the Edhrine couldn't resist the chance to humiliate them by watching them agree to surrender. They were right, but they probably did not expect the Edhrine to survive so well. He figured it was a trap when he noticed the dagger-throwers in the room. He was on guard the whole time the Sentinel leader gave his false agreement to the Edhrine's terms.

The Edhrine expected the trap and had backup waiting. Now, he had to get out of the room. He could lure the two remaining Sentinels out, and they would encounter a phalanx of men plus a few ballistae for good measure.

Thinking quickly, the Edhrine held up his dagger. It left his hand without him throwing it and went into one of the

Sentinels. The Edhrine made use of sorcery. Then, he ran at the other, using the chair as cover. The surprised Sentinel moved to the side to dodge the Edhrine. Bad move. The Edhrine extended his sword to the side and it sliced the enemy in half. The Edhrine left the room and informed his army that the "negotiations" were over. He also ordered his army to slay the rest of the Sentinel army. The sounds of battle followed the Edhrine as he walked to the ships with two men to collect a report from them.

As the Edhrine focused on the Sentinels, the admiral in his warship received information about the Edhrine's location. The admiral proceeded to follow the intelligence he received.

From the command center of his mighty warship, the admiral looked out to sea. His massive warship came across a single Sentinel ship that appeared stranded. Could it be the enemy's command ship? No. There would be another ship here, searching for survivors if that were the case.

The admiral was curious. "Prepare a boarding party. I am going personally."

The admiral left the command center without another word. When he reached the ramp, it was already lowered. The boarding party formed behind the admiral as he marched across the lowered ramp. Two Sentinels met them with weapons drawn. The admiral held up his hand, signaling his men not to attack.

"Who are you?" a Sentinel demanded.

"I am an admiral, and I have the power to destroy you. Tell me where you are going, and why you are the only ship here."

A Sentinel answered. "The Edhrine ambushed us. He killed our helmsman and then shot the wheel with a ballista. We're stuck in a circular pattern."

"Where did he go, Sentinels?"

"He went after the survivors of our forces. He should be in the Sentinels forts over there," responded the other Sentinel, pointing towards the shore.

"Thank you for the information," the admiral began. Turning to his men, he spoke again, "Execute them."

The two Sentinels fell, and admiral's catapults crushed the rest of the ship into dust.

6

The Stand

The Edhrine looked out to sea. He didn't need to wait for the silhouette in the distance to get closer to know what it was. The massive unknown warship was easily recognizable due to its size.

"On alert!" the Edhrine ordered.

The men instantly stopped celebrating their victory over the Sentinels and rushed to the ballistae. The Edhrine reviewed the options. They were effectively trapped. The warship would destroy them if they tried to escape to Sorwond or anywhere else by the sea. The only way to get out was by land. That meant leaving the ships.

The Edhrine and his men took everything they could carry and went into a Sentinel fort. They chose one far enough from the Mohraight river that the warship's catapults couldn't reach. Since the warship was still far out, the Edhrine retrieved almost everything from his ships. By the time the warship began crushing the Edhrine's ships with its catapults, even the heavy ballistae had been moved to the Sentinel fort. All the Edhrine lost was the ships themselves.

Meanwhile, the admiral listened to the report of an officer. "It is confirmed that no ballista bolts were launched at our ship during the battle, if you could even call it a battle. The enemy did not resist. Also, no corpses were found in the water, and no survivors were seen fleeing for the shore. When we searched the wreckage, we failed to find the remains of anything other than the wood of the ship itself. There was not even a cracked helmet."

The admiral spoke, "The enemy observed us at a distance and abandoned the ships. I want the chief tactical advisors summoned to the command center to have a discussion regarding their choice of attacking before confirming that the enemy was actually present."

A little while later, the tactical advisors' bodies were thrown overboard, along with the usual trash.

In a Sentinel fort, the Edhrine stood in the command center of the Sentinel fort. Ironically, it was the same fort where he previously had left the men in the prison. His forces had changed since then. Then, he led a large army. Now, he had only a half-division, but he was doing better against the Sentinels than ever before.

The Edhrine looked to the shore, where the enemy warship loomed. His ships were destroyed, and by now the enemy must have realized that the Edhrine's forces had evacuated the ships long ago. The admiral was going to have to do this on land.

In his warship, the admiral looked out. The enemy was in a Sentinel fort, for sure. He gave orders, "Deploy a scout force." The enemy wanted to test his mettle on land. The enemy would see that he was not up against an unskilled tactician. Just because he took the title of admiral did not mean he could not be a general.

The Edhrine watched as the warship reached the shore and dropped its ramps. The first wave of army of enemies marched off the ramp, holding spears and shields. The Edhrine ordered his men to advance through the foliage. They silently chipped away at the enemy's numbers. Every so often, the unknown nation's troops would find a group of their own dead, or a patrol would fail to return.

The admiral knew the enemy's strategy. They were chiseling away at his army. Eventually, this strategy would kill the entire army. Of course, that would be if the admiral didn't act. The admiral was going to act. He ordered his men to march together and search the Sentinel forts, one by one. The warship was protected, since he had nine more divisions on it.

The Edhrine watched as the enemy division marched towards the Sentinel forts. He might be outnumbered two to one, but his men were elite. The Edhrine was also a great fighter. However, that division was obviously a scouting party and not the main army.

The admiral watched from the warship as his division approached each Sentinel fort. If they found a Sentinel fort, he didn't intend to be nearby when they were slaughtered. As the admiral peered through the window, he witnessed the division being killed by arrows that came from a Sentinel fort. The admiral found his prey.

Inside the fort, the Edhrine removed his sword from a fallen Sentinel. Wave one was defeated, but there were many more to go. He looked at the warship. The Edhrine hoped that the second wave was as easy as the first.

On the warship, the admiral directed his men, "Deploy all divisions. The battle is about to begin."

The Edhrine's men looked in horror as eight full divisions

marched off the warship. They saw what appeared to be another division remaining on the ship. The Edhrine's men were grossly outnumbered. The Edhrine did the calculations. One of his men to sixteen of theirs, not counting the division remaining on the enemy ship. He would need strategy to overcome these odds, but he also did not have much time.

The admiral looked on. His divisions marched off the ramp, towards the Sentinel fort. The admiral intended to make his enemy's death slow. He would starve them out of their fort. His men would surround the enemy, and the enemy would either join the Verdarite Empire or die.

The Edhrine devised a plan. He told his men to open fire. The ballistae took out a number of men, but the ballistae would not be enough. The Edhrine needed more destructive power. He studied the warship. There was no lack of destructive power there. It was what he needed.

"Men," the Edhrine said, "keep our enemy busy. I need to speak with their leader."

His men must have thought he was a psychopath. He walked into the shadows, stealthily making his way around the battlefield. Several times along the way, he took out small groups of men before going back into the shadows. It was not long before the Edhrine reached the ramp. Now he needed to move past the division of men that guarded the warship. He noticed some windows under the huge ramps. He slipped underneath and smashed the window just by looking at it. Sorcery was a useful tool. Climbing through the window, he began the walk to the command center, wherever it was. The Edhrine hoped it was at the top of the big, obvious tower that he had seen multiple times.

Still at the Sentinel fort, Tim, the Edhrine's second-in-command was directing troops. He really hoped the Edhrine knew what he was doing. Tim had not seen the Edhrine since he left, and the men weren't doing too well.

"Sir, another wounded!" a soldier shouted.

Tim groaned and continued shooting his bow. The Edhrine needed to do this quickly. Tim mindlessly shot arrows into the horde of enemy soldiers who were ramming the gate of the fort with a sharpened log. He barely needed to aim, since they were so densely packed.

The Edhrine crept through a hallway and encountered two dead soldiers. He relaxed. The Edhrine had already been this way. He reversed direction and opened a random door. Inside was a staircase, and it only went up. The Edhrine went up stealthily. At the top was the ship's command center.

The admiral turned around, holding a dagger. "Welcome," he said, "we've been expecting you."

The admiral paused and waited for the Edhrine's reply. No reply came. Instead, the Edhrine calmly walked to the center of the command center.

"Kill him," the admiral ordered, getting impatient.

The Edhrine had the admiral's bodyguards in his peripheral vision. They wore iron armor, with navy blue markings. They also wore navy blue capes and were armed with short spears. One of the four jumped at the Edhrine. Dodging, the Edhrine slammed the bodyguard into a wall, putting him temporarily out of the fight. He stepped to the side, dodging another guard's charge. He used telekinesis to send his sword to follow the guard that ran past him. Hearing the sword impale the guard, the Edhrine rolled forward and attacked the guard he rammed into the wall first, using the guard's own spear to kill him. Two down, two to go. The other two guards charged. One pulled out a dagger and threw it. The Edhrine caught the blade and threw it back, killing the guard. Only one remained. The Edhrine did not let the extra markings on the last guard's helmet go unnoticed. This guard would be more difficult to dispatch.

The guard faced his enemy. He did not know who the enemy was, why they were hunting him, or how the enemy had gotten here. He only knew that the enemy was a threat to be eliminated, and he intended to succeed where his comrades failed. The guard went for a javelin throw. He threw his spear and then rolled to the side. He saw his spear stuck in the floor right where he was just standing. This enemy could catch projectiles. The guard rolled and retrieved his spear. He attacked the enemy, thrusting and blocking with his spear. He would finish this or die trying.

The Edhrine blocked the last guard's blows. This guard was smart. He watched how his comrades had failed, and he learned from it. He was not charging, but simply thrusting. The Edhrine decided to give the guard five more seconds of thrusting and parrying before he used one of his favorite tactics to end the man's life.

The guard was surviving. He was surprised, but he was surviving. Until he was not surviving. Without warning, the Edhrine grabbed the guard's spear in the middle of a thrust. The Edhrine thrusted the spear in the other direction, sending it through the last guard. The guard fell, revealing the admiral behind him. The admiral held a spear from one of the fallen guards. Either the admiral was desperate to defend himself or he knew how to use it.

The admiral sidestepped the Edhrine's charge, but was surprised when the Edhrine's sword went into his back. The admiral grunted, falling to one knee, and then to the ground.

The Edhrine stood over him.

"Who are you?" the fallen admiral gasped.

"I," the Edhrine proclaimed, "am the Edhrine, an Errorunsai. I would explain, but I doubt you have enough time remaining to hear my explanation."

The Edhrine did not stick around to watch the admiral die. Instead, he smashed the front window of the command center and threw the admiral out. Hopefully, someone would find the corpse and spread the news, demoralizing the entire army. Then, the Edhrine left the way he came.

Still in the middle of the battle, Tim looked on as the enemy divisions charged through the battered gate. Inside, Tim and his men made a phalanx. The enemy army would need to kill every last man to get into the fort. Tim stood on a random crate watching for ballistae or other large weapons that had the ability to reduce the phalanx to a pile of dead bodies.

Suddenly, a dead enemy soldier flew across the phalanx's field of vision. Soon, most of the enemy soldiers were looking in the direction from which the corpse had flown. Tim didn't need to guess who was there.

The Edhrine stepped in front of the broken gate, holding his sword in one hand and a very large stack of sharp rocks in the other. The rocks left the Edhrine's hand one by one, in very quick succession, impaling enemy soldiers. As the stack of rocks became a handful, the Edhrine backed through the battered gate and into the Sentinel fort. Once his left hand was empty, the Edhrine walked behind his phalanx, the men parting to allow him through.

The Edhrine heard a horn. He knew what it meant. The enemy troops turned around and ran for the ship. The Edhrine's archers killed a few, but most made it to the ship.

The Edhrine mentally laughed. He took the liberty of setting the ship on fire before he left. They weren't going to get far before the warship went up in smoke. The Edhrine set the fires in a few random storage closets. Even if they could put out the fire, the ship would still sustain extensive damage. The Edhrine also sabotaged the sails. The sails were currently down, and they weren't going back up. The warship was doomed, as were the men on it. The Edhrine watched as the oars on the bottom of the ship began to move, the men laboring to pull the ship out to sea…to its demise. The Edhrine's men celebrated on top of the Sentinel fort, watching the warship burn. It was far enough from the shore that most of the few survivors would drown. The Edhrine's men would gather the few that made it to the shore and lock them in the Sentinel fort's prison.

The warship was still moving and was not burning. Troops extinguished the fires, and they were returning to shore. The demoralizing didn't work. They retreated because they lacked a commander, and not because they were demoralized. Still, the ship moved slowly. Clearly, some oars were not working. The ship was crippled, but functional. The Edhrine watched as the ship attempted to bombard the fort from well out of range. They might not be demoralized, but they definitely had a dumb commander.

A Verdarite soldier stood in the command center. He was not a tactician. In the Verdarite Empire, two tiers in the military existed, soldiers and tacticians. The admiral was a tactician. Even so, the soldier was the highest-ranking individual remaining. His first barrage landed out of range. Perhaps that was why the admiral never ordered a barrage. Perhaps the fort was out of the warship's range. It was the only explanation for why the admiral did not order a bombardment.

The warship deployed all remaining divisions. The new commander must have been a big idiot, because there was nobody defending the ship. The Edhrine could literally walk aboard and only a skeleton crew would be there to stop him. The skeleton crew would most likely not know how to fight. Their usual jobs were rowing the ship and carrying supplies around. They would not be an issue.

A few minutes later, the Edhrine and his men crept through the woods as the soldiers of the unknown empire searched the fort they just abandoned. They had to reach the warship before the commander decided to pull back, if he was smart enough to do that. Maybe he would start searching the other forts. Either way, the Edhrine was going to get the warship for his men. Tim stood next to the Edhrine. He was the Edhrine's best soldier, and therefore the Edhrine's second-in-command. The Edhrine chose him not because he was the best duelist, as there were better duelists, but because he was the best tactician. Sure, he was not as skilled at either fighting or tactics as the Edhrine, but he was a second-in-command and not a first-in-command.

Tim looked at the Edhrine next to him. The Edhrine was walking through the brush, calm as always. Tim looked at the warship. It was on the shore, again. He saw the fire damage towards the rear of the ship. A good number of the oars were either missing or charred beyond use.

The Edhrine and his men stepped onto the ramp. They marched onboard with the enemy army oblivious to their presence. The Edhrine stepped aside to look up at the viewing window as his men marched past him. He could see the enemy commander looking down. The enemy commander was clearly a soldier. He was wearing iron armor. The Edhrine positioned himself behind the last men in the column, and they walked into the control tower.

The door to the room opened, and the Verdarite soldier turned around. The Edhrine stood with his men in a phalanx behind him. The Edhrine drew his sword. The soldier held out his. Without saying a word, they began dueling.

The Edhrine was not impressed with the soldier's skill. The Edhrine dodged the soldier's attacks, and he decided not to strike yet. He let the soldier slash at air for a little longer and then sent his sword flying. The soldier died. The Edhrine removed his sword and pointed it at the others in the room. They ran at him, despite being unarmed. The Edhrine dispatched them with ease. He then told his men that they owned the ship.

7

The Calm Before the Storm

The Edhrine's men searched the ship and didn't find any enemies near the weapons, in the chamber where the oars were stored, or on the vast deck. Although they didn't have time to check every storage room, the Edhrine knew that most of the soldiers left. This warship's primary purpose was to house the men it deployed. The admiral, his bodyguards, and a few command center personnel were the only people on board that never deployed to land.

The Edhrine met Tim at a small ballista platform. Tim informed him that the fire damage was minimal, and they could easily perform repairs once they found a city. The Edhrine thought about going to Mohraight, but that was not an option. The unknown empire almost definitely had forces there.

"Where are we going to go?" Tim asked.

"Mohraight is not an option. We can go to the Sorwondian beach, and then walk to the city from there," the Edhrine answered.

Tim asked another question, "Sorwond is pretty far inland. How are we going to move the supplies back to the ship?"

The Edhrine continued, "The unknown empire kept a lot of gold in the storage rooms. We can pay people to carry the supplies to the beach. From there, we can use the ramps to bring them up."

The Edhrine and his men rowed the warship. The Edhrine rowed for longer by using telekinesis and his muscles together. His men, unfortunately, did not have such abilities. Once close enough to reach Sorwond in small boats, the Edhrine dispatched his scouts.

The scouts returned to the warship with grave news, which they provided to Tim. "Sir, Sorwond is locked down. The Sentinels captured it. They are not letting anyone in. It seems they are anticipating an attack."

"I will inform the Edhrine," Tim announced.

After Tim provided the update, the Edhrine stepped through the door out of the command tower. His men were lined up on the deck. It looked ridiculous, half of a division standing on a deck big enough for twenty times as many men. However, he gave them credit for spreading out to take up more room.

"I am going to go on a scouting mission and will search for weak points in the wall. You will remain here. After I finish, you will stealthily attack a weak point I find. We are going to attempt to capture the Sentinel leader alive."

The Edhrine descended a staircase to some smaller landing craft. He boarded one and rowed away. The Edhrine's men left the deck and went to find something to do while their leader was scouting.

When the Edhrine arrived at the beach, he stepped out of the boat. He calmly walked towards the woods near Sorwond. Sorwond had a plain to the east and south, but the north and west were forest. The Edhrine worked best in the forest. He thought there would be few weak points on the east or south sides because that was where anyone entering the city would pass.

As the Edhrine worked his way through the forest, he thought he saw a gate in the back of the city. That was noteworthy. He continued looking through the foliage and noticed lights ahead. There was a camp. The Edhrine quickly, but silently moved through the brush until he reached several soldiers talking.

"Wait, so we need to patrol this area? I thought we need to patrol over here," a Sentinel said.

"Oh my gosh," groaned another Sentinel. Speaking louder and more angrily, he spoke again, "Xavier, we need to patrol the escape route!"

"Oh…" the Sentinel, clearly named Xavier, replied, "so we need to guard the escape route so people can get out in the event of a siege, or food can get in if we want."

"Yes," the other soldier confirmed.

"Xavier!" a distant voice shouted.

"Coming!" Xavier shouted nervously. He got up and sprinted away from the campfire, towards a makeshift watch tower about thirty yards away.

The Edhrine stepped out of the bush. The three men who remained at the campfire looked up, only to be pummeled by small, sharp rocks flying out of the Edhrine's hand. The Edhrine was not incredibly skilled with telekinesis, but he was good enough. The Edhrine slipped back into the foliage, waiting for the other soldier, Xavier, to return.

Xavier walked out of the watch tower. His commander yelled at him for patrolling the wrong area, and now he was demoted. He looked at the rank insignia on his shoulder. Soon, he would be going to a lesser unit. He walked into the camp. The fire was extinguished and all the other men were laying down.

"Are you guys sleeping on the job?" Xavier questioned.

The men didn't move.

"All right, you can stop now. I know you're faking it."

Suddenly, he heard a twig crack. He tensed. Instinctively, he pulled out his crossbow. He heard another twig crack and began to tremble. He felt the crossbow fire and the bolt disappeared into a bush. He frantically pulled another arrow from his quiver, but before he could load it, he froze. Walking out of the bushes was the Edhrine, holding the crossbow bolt that he accidentally fired. Before Xavier could say anything, that arrow left the Edhrine's hand and killed him.

Back in the warship, Tim sat at a table in the barracks. This ship had barracks big enough for ten divisions, so the half-division of the Edhrine's men claimed bunks near the door and made fortifications in case enemy soldiers were hiding in the vast room.

"Darn it!" Tim exclaimed.

Tim watched as a soldier claimed the extra meal ration from the center of the table. He and his men were playing a game with the winner getting an extra ration. Tim was hungry, but he didn't want to walk all the way to the food storage room. Unfortunately, he would have to. He and the other losers got up and walked through the hallway to the ration storage room.

Tim walked back from the ration storage room. When he returned to the bunks, he saw the other soldiers leaving. They were going towards the deck, so Tim followed. He knew the Edhrine was probably about to give orders as it happened every time the Edhrine called them to the deck.

The Edhrine stood outside the door to the command center. His men positioned themselves on the deck in front of him.

Tim walked up to the Edhrine and said, "Sir, everyone is present."

"Good," the Edhrine announced, "I found something of note. There is a back gate that faces north. That is our target. From what I can tell, the Sentinels were planning to use it to smuggle in food supplies in the event of a siege. That implies they have enough soldiers to be comfortable with a siege. We will need to be creative. I plan to enter the city and, as I said earlier, capture their leader alive. If that succeeds, we can force them to surrender."

The Edhrine entered the command center without another word. Once sure that the Edhrine was not returning with additional instructions, the soldiers left to pack some rations and prepare for battle.

8

The Siege

The Edhrine's men silently moved through the foliage. They were well-trained. The Edhrine heard two sticks hit each other. That was the signal. The other group was in position. The Edhrine grabbed two sticks and did the same. With that, the two groups rushed out and the six Sentinels guarding the gate fell to the ground, dead. The Edhrine's men retrieved their thrown daggers and arrows and then looked to the gate. The Edhrine took the dead Sentinels and hid them in the woods. He walked up to the gate with a rope that had a hook on one end. He used telekinesis to send the rope to the top of the wall, and the hook caught something. The Edhrine and his men climbed up the rope to the top of the wall and climbed down the other side just as fast. If a guard spotted them on the wall, the attack was over.

The Edhrine motioned for his men to get inside of a building. His men entered and found the building to be empty.

Tim looked at the Edhrine and asked, "How did you know?"

"I read the sign on the door. This building is a storehouse," the Edhrine answered.

"Why is it empty, then?"

The Edhrine glanced at Tim. Tim quickly realized that the Sentinels had raided the place and all that remained were a few empty crates and a random dagger on the floor. The Edhrine and his men reviewed the plan for attacking the main citadel. That was where the leader would be, because that was where the leader always was.

The Edhrine led his men through the streets. They bought disguises from a merchant, being sure to pay him for his silence. After all, he did see a bunch of strange people in full combat gear ask to buy cloaks. There weren't many reasons why that would happen. The merchant's silence was crucial.

Inside the Sorwondian citadel, the Sentinel commander was seated on the throne of Sorwond. All previous members of the royal family were dead. He had found a base. Why did he need a base? Because he was starting a rebellion against the actual Sentinels. The real Sentinels refused to ally with the Verdarite Empire. They were fools. This Sentinel would complete the alliance, and show those false Sentinels exactly why they should have joined. As a Sentinel entered the room, the commander stood.

"Report," the commander ordered.

"I have the report written, in here," the Sentinel replied, holding up a sack.

"Is this some kind of joke?" the commander questioned.

Without warning, the Sentinel pulled a spear out of the sack. "I advise that you remain in place," the disguised soldier warned.

"Who are you?" the commander demanded.

Suddenly, a voice spoke from behind him, "We are your enemies."

The commander turned, and found himself staring into a

black cloth. He stepped backwards, disturbed by how easily the Edhrine had snuck up behind him. Two soldiers came out from behind the Edhrine holding rope.

"Who are you?" the commander asked, now looking at the Edhrine.

"Tie him to a support pillar," the Edhrine directed.

The soldiers tied him securely. They stepped back and pulled out bows, drawing them back and aiming them at the commander's head.

"Who are you?" the Edhrine countered.

"I am a commander of a unit of true Sentinels. If you are an enemy of the false ones, we have no reason to fight. We can both join the Verdarite—"

"Who are the Verdarites?" the Edhrine questioned, interrupting him.

The commander realized the Edhrine was an enemy of the Sentinels for a reason other than the Verdarite issue.

"The Verdarite Empire is an expansive empire. We met one of their admirals. The Sentinel leaders refused his offer to join. I, at the time a low-ranking soldier, and many others deserted and hid in the wild. In time, I was appointed the leader. If the old Sentinels had a problem with you, we were never informed. It was Sentinel protocol. They tell a new soldier who the other nations are, but they don't tell him who is friendly and who is an enemy. Then, one day, the new soldier is told one or two of the enemies and sometimes an ally. The new soldier is then sent to war."

The Edhrine spoke again, "That explains how you did not recognize me. Unfortunately, you were affiliated with the Sentinels, who are enemies of mine. Ever since their first unprovoked attacks, we have been at war. Since you claim to be attempting to change the Sentinel leadership, not destroy the Sentinels, you are still my enemy."

"I protest! I am not allied with the Sentinels nearly as much as I am with the Verdari—"

"The Verdarites are enemies of mine as well. Their admiral tried to eliminate us without our aggression. You are allied with two enemy factions. As we speak, my men are informing your soldiers of your capture. They have been forced to surrender, which only grows our number of hostages. The city is ours, Sentinel. Since you are all captives, I will not kill you. You will be sent into the nearby Centaur Woods."

"What? That's a death sentence! The centaurs kill everyone who goes there!" the commander protested.

"Believe me, if you are resourceful enough to ally with the Verdarites, you will at least be able to negotiate with the centaurs," the Edhrine told the commander.

The Edhrine heard swords clashing. He calmly walked to a balcony and peered down as his men completely destroyed the Sentinels who refused to surrender. None of the Edhrine's five men had fallen, yet the ten Sentinels were all dead. He turned and ordered his men to ready the new prisoners for the Centaur Woods.

The Edhrine's men escorted the prisoners to the edge of the woods, where they left them. The Edhrine's men ordered the Sentinels not to move until the Edhrine and his men were out of sight. Most of the Sentinels obeyed. They were also instructed not to head towards Sorwond. A few Sentinels disobeyed that command, and they were quite surprised to find the Edhrine waiting there with his army. Those Sentinels quickly changed their minds and retreated.

Some time later, the Edhrine sat upon the throne of Sorwond.

He knew that controlling the city would be beneficial, but he also knew it could draw unwanted attention. While he maintained the illusion that he would remain in Sorwond indefinitely, he really just wanted to complete the repairs to his warship and get out. The Edhrine knew he would not be able to protect the city in the event of a siege. It was one of the disadvantages of having a small group of elites. A small group of elites wouldn't be able to defend a fortress-city made for armies.

When the repairs finished on his ship, the Edhrine was happy his stay in Sorwond was over. He wanted to leave before the Sentinels inevitably came, and get back to hunting them. This time, however, he had a large warship and enough men to use the weapons. The ship was not ideal for a militia of the size the Edhrine's, but it had catapults. Even if he only had a few men, it translated to a few giant boulders crushing the enemy.

The Edhrine boarded the ramp with his men. He marched on board, leaving Sorwond without a ruler. He did not turn around to look back at the city as he walked to the command tower.

9

The Infiltration

Verdar VI, emperor of the Verdarite Empire, sat upon his throne. He looked down upon the man standing before him. Well, he used to be a man. He was a man just like any other Verdarite, until the Empire moved to this dark region. Now, every Verdarite was either a manipulative, strategic tactician or a brainless, strong foot soldier. Or, like Verdar VI, they were politicians. However, there was not much in the way of politics in the Verdarite Empire. They were all enslaved to the evil power lurking within the dark area they inhabited, but they were too blind to see that. They saw an impregnable position from which they could launch a conquest on the entire world.

Verdar VI looked down at the man, and spoke. "You are now an admiral of the Verdarite Empire. Leave here…Admiral IV."

None of the people in the Verdarite Empire used names. The emperors simply used the name Verdar, after the empire's founder, and then a number that indicated how many generations away from Verdar they were. The top military strategists used their rank and then a number based on how many others of that rank already existed. Now, Verdar VI appointed another admiral, to replace the previous Admiral IV, who died. The new Admiral IV left the room, ready to claim his new warship. The new warship had an identifier, too. It was A-5. The 'A' was for admiral, because it was the type of ship an admiral commanded, and it was 5 because it was the fifth one built.

Admiral IV did not just have a standard admiral's warship. His warship was the prototype of a newer, compact version. Some soldiers thought the warship was inferior because of the size difference, but there was a reason they were soldiers and not tacticians. Admiral IV used to correct them when he was a lower rank, but no longer. They usually forgot about it the next day, and he would correct them again, telling them the benefits of a more compact and inexpensive design. He made prototypes since before he earned a rank that came with a number.

A long voyage later, Admiral IV peered out the window. The city of Sorwond, the last location of his target, stood before him. It was in flames. A force of Sentinels fought with a force of rebel Sentinels. Admiral IV refrained from intervening, despite his soldiers' desire to do so. The rebel Sentinels were pro-Verdarite, but Admiral IV had no business helping them. The Verdarite Empire didn't need the Sentinels, and if they did, Admiral IV wasn't going to be the one to get them on the Verdarites' side.

Admiral IV had what he needed from Sorwond and set sail. Just as the previous Admiral IV followed rumors regarding the enemy's whereabouts, the new Admiral IV did, too. There was a rumor that the Edhrine had been in Sorwond. He went there, and inquired. He left Sorwond leaving a dead Sorwondian merchant and bringing along some newfound knowledge. The merchant witnessed the enemy take over Sorwond, and was paid to not tell the Sentinels about the strike. Of course, the

Verdarites were not the Sentinels, and the Edhrine finished his attack, so the merchant wasn't breaking any promises. The merchant became interested once he learned that the enemy's attack succeeded, which wasn't long after he sold the cloaks to the enemy's men. He found out that the enemy had a huge warship that was an older model of the standard Verdarite admiral's warship. The merchant explained that he saw the ship moving slowly in a direction very close to due west. Admiral IV did not know how far out the enemy had traveled, but he had a precise direction.

After getting the information, Admiral IV offered to pay the merchant a Verdarite dagger in exchange for the information. He thought the deal was more than fair. Admiral IV handed the dagger towards the merchant handle first, and suddenly turned it the other way and thrusted the blade straight into the merchant's stomach. "You can keep that," said Admiral IV has he walked away, not bothering to retrieve the dagger.

In his warship, the Edhrine looked out to sea. The Sentinels were going to leave him alone, for now. The Edhrine resupplied his ship, and he would not need to resupply again for a while. He decided to return to the Sentinel forts north of the Edhormond Mountains. He and his men took the food supplies from the forts and lived on the ship. The Edhrine confirmed that no enemies survived in any of the ship's numerous rooms, unless they were skilled enough to evade his troops' multiple sweeps. The Edhrine used some supplies from the Sentinel fort to create a rowing system. It was not automatic. Rather, it utilized a system of pullies to pull the oars back and forth. The pully system made the rowing easier, and he needed only four strong rowers. The Edhrine divided his half-division into five groups. During travel, the groups would swap between the different assignments of rowing and patrolling.

The Edhrine remained focused on the sea. He spotted something coming. The shape of the craft was unfamiliar, but unmistakably a warship. However, unlike most warships, this one had a short command tower. The Edhrine was impressed. Someone finally designed a ship that didn't waste wood on what was essentially a staircase. Tall command towers didn't give the ship much of a tactical advantage because the raised command towers never had weapons.

Admiral IV could see his prey ahead. The enemy warship faced towards Sorwond, which meant it was directly facing Admiral IV. The admiral carefully proceeded from this direction. Like most warships, the weapons were on the sides. Therefore, the enemy would need to turn to open fire. Of course, that would alert Admiral IV that the enemy was going to attack, and his prototype could turn faster than the bulky, inefficient model of the enemy. He also had many more men. If the ship left Sorwond at a crawl, that meant that few men were using the oars. Not only would the enemy have a hard time moving, but they would not be able to operate all of the warship's weapons. Admiral IV had neither of those disadvantages. This fight would be anything but fair.

The Edhrine ordered his men to turn the ship's side to the approaching ship well before it was in firing range. He couldn't assess the ship's likely weaknesses from such a distance, but if the rest of the ship was designed as efficiently as the command tower, he could make an educated guess. As he watched the ship, the ship continued forward and did not turn sideways. The Edhrine realized the tactic before the ship reached ramming speed.

"Move forward! They're trying to ram us," the Edhrine yelled.

The men rushed from the catapult stations to the pulley-operated oars. The Edhrine dodged the ramming attack with a quick 90-degree turn to the right. The enemy ship suddenly stopped. The Edhrine knew what the enemy was planning next.

Admiral IV's favorite maneuver worked. He already knew that the enemy was quite a tactician, so he made a ramming maneuver that was just noticeable enough. The enemy initiated a turn, and Admiral IV stopped right when the enemy was to his side. Now, Admiral IV had his ship's side to the enemy, but the enemy had their ship's rear to the admiral.

"Open fire!" Admiral IV commanded.

The Edhrine decided to try something risky and directed the men to move the ship towards the enemy.

One of the Edhrine's men responded, "Sir, we will have to turn around. They will destroy us by the time our side is to them."

"I meant to move in reverse," the Edhrine explained.

The crew in the command center looked at the Edhrine like he was insane and then relayed the order down to the oarsmen.

Admiral IV watched as the enemy ship reversed towards him. What were they thinking? He decided against maintaining the bombardment. If the enemy was trying something, it clearly relied on their current position, and if Admiral IV could prevent it, he would do all he could. He ordered his ship to move in reverse, too, which put him safely to the side of the enemy's route. He then directed his men to rotate and align the side of his ship with the enemy.

The Edhrine watched as the enemy moved. His plan had mostly worked. He got the enemy to halt the bombardment, but the enemy was not going to fall for their own trick. They were sure to angle their side to the Edhrine, so they could fire back if the Edhrine stopped. The Edhrine instead ordered his men to ignore all distractions, and do all they could to successfully ram the enemy. The Edhrine knew that ramming would not destroy the enemy warship and would do equal damage to both ships, but the Edhrine was not trying to damage the ship. He was going to board it.

Admiral IV looked on as the enemy attempted ram his ship. The enemy was noticeably failing. However, because of the constant evasive maneuvers, A-5 could not launch a barrage at the enemy ship. All attempts resulted in wasted ammunition, and Admiral IV did not want to waste anything. He decided to play the enemy's game, for now.

The Edhrine's men were not skilled at ramming, but it didn't matter to the Edhrine. They were making the enemy unprepared for the Edhrine's real attempt. Since Plan B, which was ramming and boarding, didn't work, the Edhrine would revert to Plan A, which was bombarding. Without warning, the Edhrine stopped the ship and opened fire on a surprised enemy. The Edhrine directed his men to aim for the enemy catapult and ballista platforms.

Admiral IV was surprised. He had to admit that the enemy was a good tactician, but the effort would ultimately be futile. Admiral IV possessed more weapons, and the Edhrine could not destroy all of them before A-5 turned its side to the Edhrine's ship.

The Edhrine timed his move. When the enemy was almost facing him, the Edhrine moved. The Verdarites fired their barrage of stones too early. Clearly, the Verdarite ship could use a crew with a better reaction time. The rocks from the Verdarite catapults hit the water behind him. Only a few of the flying projectiles hit the back of the Edhrine's ship. The Edhrine ordered his own barrage. Thanks to the Verdarite's bad reaction time, the barrage hit. He saw the holes in the enemy ship created by stones. Since he needed to spread out his men, the Edhrine preferred to use smaller rocks, rather than large ones. The large ones required multiple men to carry, and therefore multiple men per catapult. A single person could load the smaller rocks onto a catapult. Additionally, the catapults could fit more than one small stone.

A man ran into the command center and reported to the Edhrine, "Sir, that catapult shot penetrated all the way through our ship! It went all the way through the bottom. We're sinking."

The Edhrine told the man to inform his soldiers to return to the oars. He said they were going to try to ram one last time. The Edhrine faced his ship towards the enemy ship and advanced.

Admiral IV saw the enemy's attempt to ram. They must be sinking. The enemy was unable to ram last time, so it was unlikely he would succeed this time. Admiral IV decided to open fire and tear the ship apart as it attempted to ram. He made sure to adjust his ship's position. He knew that all of the Edhrine's men were rowing, and the chance that someone was watching where they were going were slim. The enemy would go past A-5, and they would be vulnerable to bombardment.

The Edhrine peered through a slit in the front of the ship. How did anyone navigate with these? The bottom of the ship, where the oars were, had a slit for someone to look through to make sure they were going the right direction. The Edhrine decided to come down there and help guide his ramming attempt. He hoped his previous failed ramming attempts would create a false sense of security.

Admiral IV watched. The enemy did not change its heading. Obviously, nobody was navigating. He observed as boulders and stones sank deep into the enemy ship, causing significant damage. At the last minute, the enemy warship turned and was on a course that would ram straight into A-5.

Admiral IV gave orders, "Aim for the bow of their ship. They will not ram unless they can do so without destroying their ship." Even though he said that, the admiral doubted it. The enemy would sink even if they didn't do something. If they could sink the other ship, too, they would.

The Edhrine smiled under his helmet as the enemy ship made a futile attempt to move out of the way. The Edhrine ran away from the front of his ship to avoid the impending impact. Soon enough, his ship smashed into the side of the enemy ship. He turned around and drew his sword. He and his men moved through a hole in the wall, jumping across a small gap over the ocean into another hole in the enemy ship's wall. The Edhrine and his men were in.

Admiral IV watched as an entire division of his men attempted to use spears to move the enemy warship. The admiral had not given orders to try that, but he wasn't going to stop them until he needed them. They were trying to pry the enemy warship out of A-5's side. Unfortunately, that would require much more power than a division's worth of muscles. Their effort resulted in more broken spears than inches of the enemy ship moved.

Snapping out of his amusement, Admiral IV told the division to stop trying to complete an impossible task and start doing something important. Admiral IV expected the enemy to try to make it to the command center. However, he still deployed some forces onto the enemy warship. The enemy had made a bad move. If they wanted to strand the admiral's soldiers on their sinking ship, they would have to somehow dislodge the iron bow from A-5's side.

The Edhrine looked around the enemy ship. He and his men decided to stow away in a storage room that appeared to be seldom used. He knew this admiral was not stupid. He doubted that the security on the command center would be nearly as bad as the other Verdarite admiral's.

Admiral IV received his report. The soldiers said that the enemy was not on board the enemy ship, A-4, and if they were, they were good at their job, because they evaded a bow-to-stern sweep made by five divisions. Admiral IV looked out the window down at the deck of his own ship. He knew the enemy was on board his ship. If the divisions searched A-4 so quickly, how much faster would they completely search A-5, the small compact ship.

The Edhrine and his men hid in crates. The Edhrine knew the enemy would search the Edhrine's warship, and find nobody in it, very quickly. He also knew they would sweep their own ship next. The crates were uncomfortable, but they had survival supplies in them. The Edhrine and his men could survive for weeks and not have to get out of the crates.

Admiral IV received an updated report; nobody was on board A-4 or A-5. Every dusty storage room was checked. Unless the enemy disappeared into the walls, there was no possibility they were here...or was there? The admiral would need to think about this.

The Edhrine knew the searches were over. He heard the men come in and check behind all the crates. Luckily, they didn't think to check inside the crates. The Edhrine got out of his crate and his soldiers did the same. They looked at the door. Nobody there. The Edhrine then had them make a "room" out of crates in the back and a "hallway" that allowed access into it. The crate "fort" did not have a ceiling, but it was tall enough to hide the men. If they were discovered, they could hold out there for longer than they could without the fort. The Edhrine moved most of the survival supplies into the room. He also covered the entryway with a spare cloak. It didn't look out of place, considering how much random junk was already lying around in there.

Admiral IV thought. There were many hiding spots on A-5, and he couldn't afford to check them all. He needed to lure them out. Or, he could starve them out. There were a few storage rooms with food that could be secured, and then the soldiers could guard the hallways and the outside of the other rooms. However, that plan would take too long, and he would have failed his first mission for not meeting the deadline. He had just recently got promoted. This was his mission, and he would complete it. He had to draw them out, somehow.

From the storage room, the Edhrine and his men watched Verdarite patrolmen performing a search. The Edhrine debated whether it was worthwhile to kill them. Both options had their pros and cons. However, he realized the value of the patrolmen's armor. He made his decision. Jumping out of his crate, the Edhrine drew his sword and jumped at the enemies. He slew one after the other, and his men came out to join him. Once the patrolmen were all dead, the Edhrine told his men to put on the patrolmen's armor and put their old armor on the dead bodies. They grabbed the dead soldiers and dragged them down the hall, on the way to the command center.

Admiral IV heard a voice coming through the intercom tubes,

which traversed the ship to enable communication. The voice said, "Sir, we found the enemies we were searching for. One of them is alive. We have him as a prisoner."

The Edhrine's plan involved pretending to be a prisoner. It was easier than trying to wear a disguise, since he didn't have to worry about the black cloth in his helmet visor, and he had a reason to be there. Now, he and several of his men were outside the command center. Because there weren't enough disguises for everyone, a few men stayed in the storage room. One of the disguised men spoke into the intercom tube, and they waited for the doors to open. When the doors opened, the Edhrine observed a soldier standing next to an intercom tube. The intercom tube must have connected to the command center. After going through several more doors, the Edhrine concluded that the doors opened when the soldiers behind them unlocked them, and they only unlocked them with orders from the command center.

Admiral IV watched as the soldiers marched up with the prisoner between them. The prisoner's hands were tied behind his back.

"So, your plan has failed?" the admiral asked while pacing.

The Edhrine answered, "It would appear so."

The admiral spoke again, "Do you know what my mission was?"

"It was either to kill me or to capture me."

"Both of those assumptions are false. The mission was to eliminate your faction, and I succeeded very well in doing so."

"You seem to easily forget the contributions of the previous admiral."

"He failed his mission, and Verdar will not care if I take credit."

The Edhrine guessed that Verdar was their leader.

"Credit does not concern me. What I wanted to do was protect the people under me. You are preventing me from doing that, so I will have to kill you," the Edhrine threatened.

The admiral chuckled, "You are not in a position to do that."

"Guess again," the Edhrine replied, slipping his hands out of the loose knots and taking his sword from one of his disguised men.

"Kill him!" the admiral ordered, expecting the Edhrine's captors to engage.

They didn't. Instead, they raised their spears toward the admiral and the other Verdarites in the command center.

The Edhrine raised his sword to point at the admiral's chest. "I think your tactics could use improvement. You demonstrate great tactical aptitude in large battles, but you are clearly unfamiliar with small, elite groups such as mine. Numbers are not everything, admiral."

The Edhrine's men tied up the entire command center crew. The doors to the command center were locked, and nobody opened them without a direct order from the command center. The command center would definitely not be opening any doors for the Verdarites.

Tim removed his heavy Verdarite helmet as soon as the command center was secured. He had no clue how anyone could be comfortable with such heavy armor.

The Edhrine spoke into an intercom tube and ordered the crew to pry his old ship, apparently called A-4, from the side of his new one. It took a lot of effort, but the entire Verdarite crew managed to pry it out.

The Edhrine told his men that he wouldn't be able to command the enemies for long before the enemies grew suspicious. Besides, someone would have to deliver food to the command center for them and the Verdarites would be suspicious the second someone saw the captured crew. They would need to hide the crew. The Edhrine had the perfect plan. He took the captured crew and hid them under spare cloaks, gagging them to prevent them from making noise. He then sent some of his men to get food supplies and move as many rations as they could to the command center. The Edhrine issued some "admiral's orders" detailing a strategy in case of an attack. The whole thing was just an excuse to move supplies to the command center. They could survive on this ship as long as they weren't fighting Verdarites. The Edhrine realized that he could carry on his campaign against the Sentinels by pitting this Verdarite warship against them.

10

The Aggressors

The Sentinel ruler surveyed the others around him. They agreed that the Edhrine posed a problem. Ever since that one raid against them, the Edhrine was out for revenge. Maybe he had an excuse as to why it wasn't revenge, but that's what it seemed to the Sentinel ruler. The ruler spoke, "We cannot commit a task force to the Edhrine. We have more issues with the Verdarites and the rebels. The rebels eliminated our spies in Sorwond, and now we do not have any influence there. The Verdarites engaged our forces in the Elemental Mountains, and a few men went missing when exploring the volcano. There are too many enemies attacking us."

The Sentinel ruler zoned out as his underlings argued about logistics and then which target was most important. Once he snapped back to the discussion, they finally decided the argument was worthless and that they should vote on the most important target with each cause getting a division for each vote it got. The Sentinel ruler approved. Not surprisingly, the Edhrine received the most votes. Second was the Sentinel rebels, and then the Verdarites. The Edhrine would have a fun time with the fleet coming his direction.

Just before the Sentinel spies in Sorwond were eliminated, they had learned that the Edhrine was near Complex 6. Complex 6 was the fort complex north of the Edhormond Mountains. The Edhrine was there before he was defeated near the Sacred River. That attack reduced the Edhrine's militia to a mere half division. Unfortunately, that wasn't the end of him.

Back on A-5, the Edhrine spotted multiple shapes closing in on the horizon. They were warships. The Edhrine hoped they weren't Verdarite. He turned to the intercom tubes and announced, "Battle stations! Unidentified ships coming in from the south!" As the ships got closer, the Edhrine revised his message, "These are Sentinel warships. Angle our side to them and prepare to fire." The Edhrine really wanted to tell his men to open fire, but if the Verdarites weren't already at war with the Sentinels, those on the ship would get extremely suspicious.

The Sentinel admiral heard his officer tell him that the ship was Verdarite. He had him repeat the message to be sure he didn't mishear it. The Edhrine lost a battle! He was gone! The Verdarites vanquished him. His ship had sunk and the Verdarites controlled the area here. Then, he stopped celebrating when he realized he had to use these small Sentinel ships to board a Verdarite warship. Protocol dictated that if your target is absent, either retreat or fight the nearest enemy. The Sentinel admiral chose the latter. He knew there was no escaping the Verdarites. He would fight them to the end.

The Edhrine ordered "his" crew to open fire the second he saw the Sentinel fleet rushing towards them. He knew he had a problem. Sure, this warship could crush those types of ships, but there were a lot of them, and they were all coming to ram his ship. He might be able to destroy half using large stones, but the other half would ram. He gave the best order possible. "Open fire, and do not retreat! Fight for the Verdarites!" Ordinarily, he would launch as many stones as possible and then abandon ship, but he was commanding enemies. He wanted to get them killed.

As the Edhrine predicted, the stones crippled the first half of the Sentinel ships. They were either sinking and unable to move fast enough to ram or just split in half altogether. The Edhrine did not order the Verdarites to stop firing when the second half of Sentinel ships began approaching. Nonetheless, trying to shoot all of them was like trying to block an arrow rain with a small shield. The remaining Sentinel ships crashed into the side of A-5. The Edhrine maintained his balance. He watched the Sentinels jump on board and slaughter the Verdarite soldiers manning the catapults. The Sentinels began searching the ship. The Edhrine relayed orders. He positioned the soldiers on board to fight the Sentinels. It seemed evil, trying to get as many of the participants of the battle killed as possible, but it was ultimately to protect his men. If the Verdarites and Sentinels fell, then they couldn't attack his men. That was what he wanted. He watched as the Verdarites and Sentinels clashed on the deck, killing each other and giving the Edhrine an easier time. The Edhrine was not surprised when the last of the Verdarites fell. The Sentinels may have worse ships, but they had no shortage of men.

The Sentinels marched to the command tower. It was time to give those strong security doors a test. When they arrived at the tower, they were polite enough to speak into the intercom tube. "Greetings, Verdarite admiral. We are here to demand your surrender. We can hear you on the other side of the doors."

The Edhrine chuckled to himself. He was not a Verdarite, and about ten doors stood in between him and the Sentinels. They must have heard the Verdarite behind the door. The Edhrine told the soldiers at the doors to remain strong and not to open the doors. He returned to the intercom tube that connected to the Sentinels. "This is the Edhrine. I am not surrendering, and I am also not on the other side of that door."

The Sentinels began ramming at the security doors like their lives depended on it. They hated the Edhrine more than the Verdarites. He listened as the Sentinels wasted their energy, ramming through the doors. At last, the exhausted Sentinels ran into the command center. The first wave, the ones who were ramming, fell as soon as they entered. The Edhrine's men readied their bows, and were careful to remain behind the makeshift cover they set up.

The Edhrine stood in front of his men. A few Sentinels attempted to throw projectiles, but the Edhrine either caught or dodged the projectiles. He was getting better with his sorcery. However, he knew he could not hold out in the command center forever. Eventually, the Sentinels would just torch the ship, and he would have no way to escape. He motioned his men up, and they began going through the hallways, towards the Sentinel ships.

Tim marched behind the Edhrine. He could see the door that went out of the command tower. They would exit to the deck, in front of all the Sentinel ships. Tim watched as the Edhrine pushed the large door open. He stood, silent. Tim and the other soldiers rushed in front of him, raising their weapons.

The Edhrine saw the wave of his men rush past him and form a loose perimeter. He turned his head towards the Sentinels who rushed toward him. It was time to fight. The Edhrine pulled out a pouch he had on his hip. He opened it and poured the sharp pebbles inside into his hand. The first wave of Sentinels fell to the barrage of telekinetically launched projectiles. The Edhrine knew he would need to retreat once the main Sentinel force became aware of them.

A Sentinel commander rushed off his ship. He could see... the Edhrine? What was the Edhrine doing on a Verdarite ship? They couldn't be allies. Had the Edhrine killed scores of Verdarites? Did he stow away? It didn't matter. The commander and his division charged forward.

The Edhrine saw the incoming division at the far end of the deck. He ordered his men to retreat inside the command tower. They took up defensive positions. Rather conveniently, the entrance to the short command tower contained cover and fortifications for defenders. The designer of this ship took every possibility, even boarding, into consideration.

The Sentinel commander reached the door. Two of his men pulled the door open, while the rest charged in. They regretted it for the few seconds before they were dead. There were hiding places and even miniature walls inside the lower part of the command tower. Sure, the command tower was short, but it was still big enough for some impressive defenses. Arrows were flying out of the windows. Yes, there were windows in the walls and defenses. The room had another door at the far end, which led to the command center. The Sentinel commander just finished processing all of this when an arrow sent him falling to the ground along with the other Sentinels.

The Edhrine watched as the Sentinels fell to the arrows. The room was designed in such a way where the Edhrine had nearly every advantage except for numbers. The division of Sentinels fell before the wooden battlements and miniature ballista emplacements within minutes.

The Edhrine still had to deal with a lot more Sentinels, and some of them would be coming from behind the defenses. That was the weak point. The defenses were all hollow, with openings in the rear. It was likely designed to prevent enemies that advanced beyond this point from using the defenses against forces from inside the ship. Unfortunately, the ship designer didn't account for invaders that could come from that direction. The Edhrine told his men march to behind him as he looked for the nearest Sentinel ship to capture. He needed to get off of A-5. He chuckled to himself. The admiral would be disappointed when he finds out that his glorious warship had a bunch of Sentinel warships stuck in the side of it and that the Edhrine left a deadly parting gift. The Edhrine and his men rushed onto a Sentinel warship and rowed it out of the side of A-5. Then, Tim and a few men threw torches onto the deck of A-5. Sure, someone would see it, but the Sentinels and Verdarites would be more worried about each other than the fire. They couldn't take care of both.

The Edhrine won the day. He was alive, and so were his men.

11

The Last Battle

The Mokror and the Ifloract stood at a table in the Depths of Flame, the Ifloract's home. The Mokror used a dagger to carve her name into the obsidian shard, signing the agreement with the Ifloract. The Verdarite Empire was clearly utilizing dark sorcery and becoming corrupted by it. They would have to go to their lands and destroy the Verdarites. Still, they wondered how to best eliminate them. Perhaps the land corrupted them. If so, none of the Errorunsai's armies could go inside. That would create more problems. Still, there were two other Errorunsai to get on board. They could already guess the one who was less likely to join the alliance.

Far away from the Depths of Flame, the Edhrine and his men sailed away in the Sentinel warship. The Edhrine was going to Mohraight. He had stolen a Sentinel warship, but it would not help him unless he added ballistae. While Mohraight was not a place he could fight Sentinels, it was his best chance to get the modifications. However, the Verdarites controlled Mohraight. The Edhrine would have a fight on his hands to get his modifications. Either that or he could try to use stealth. He would make that decision when he arrived.

Some time later, the Mokror watched a Sentinel ship going through the Mohraight Graveyard. She knew that only the Edhrine was skilled, and crazy, enough to navigate a ship through there. She got on a raft and rowed out. She needed to get a better boat. Going through the water on these makeshift rafts was near-impossible.

The Edhrine spotted a raft approaching the ship from behind. He didn't need to guess its occupant. He ordered his men to stop and allow the Mokror to come aboard.

"What brings you to the Mohraight Graveyard?" the Mokror asked, sitting inside the command center across from the Edhrine. She had been courteous enough not to bring her spiders. The Edhrine's men were grateful for that.

The Edhrine answered, "I am going to Mohraight, and this is the most efficient way to get there."

The Mokror continued, "I will get straight to the point, since that is how you like your information. The Ifloract and I are making an alliance against the Verdarites. We have strong reason to believe that they are being manipulated by an evil sorcery. We do not know much, but we know that their activities have been consistent with ancient prophecies about a dark empire. We need to defeat them, and we are trying to bring the Errorunsai against them."

The Edhrine responded, "The Verdarites are enemies of mine, but I am currently at war with the Sentinels. My men will not be safe until they are destroyed."

"What makes you say that? The Verdarites are more powerful than the Sentinels, and they, too, are after you."

"The Verdarites are not putting all of their effort against me. If they can produce warships as quickly as they evidently can, they would be able to defeat me in any naval battle. Think about it. They lost one massive warship only to create another almost instantly. If they wanted me dead as much as you say, they would have warships patrolling the entire Mohraight River."

"They don't want you dead for any reason other than that you have the capacity to resist them. Believe me, once they finish the Sentinels and the other major nations, they are going to start going after small groups like yours. They have already conquered most of the North Morhor Plain, enslaving tribesmen there for an unknown purpose. We're not sure where they have taken them. If they can so effectively take over an entire region of warlike tribes, they could do the same to the major nations and you."

"Your arguments are persuasive, I must admit, but they are not persuasive enough. The Sentinels are committing their full effort against me and the Verdarites are not. The Sentinels are currently the major threat to me. I will consider joining your alliance against the Verdarites as soon as the Sentinels are eliminated."

"The Verdarites will be too strong for us by then. Regardless, you stated your choice. I will tell the Ifloract." With that, the Mokror departed.

The Edhrine left the command center and went to the bow of the ship. He saw the Mokror's raft returning to the island. Once she was out of sight, he directed his men to continue to Mohraight. Maybe he wasn't joining the anti-Verdarite alliance, but he did need a place to repair, and Mohraight was the best coastal city for that.

At the Mokror's island, the Mokror and the Ifloract met again. The Ifloract made no comment as his fiery glow illuminated the dark, filthy passages. The Mokror walked beside him.

"The Edhrine refused to join. He says the Sentinels are more of a concern," the Mokror told the Ifloract.

The Ifloract replied, "I had little success with the Marantaur. Namely, I couldn't find him. He usually hangs out somewhere in the North Morhor Plain, but since the Verdarites took over, he's gone underground."

The Mokror continued, "This alliance is going to just be us. It is a shame that we don't have the Edhrine's tactical skill. He could probably lead us to victory with just the forces we have."

"Yes, but he will not be joining us. We will need to manage on our own."

At Mohraight, the Edhrine looked out toward the water at the edge of Mohraight. There were a lot of smaller ships, about the size of a Sentinel warship. There was a large warship, too, which looked like A-5. Another admiral was there, and strange banners hung on all the Mohraight buildings. The banners were red, and they depicted a war hammer. That certainly represented the Verdarites well. The Edhrine studied the situation from his Sentinel ship. His men extinguished all the lamps, and the ship became virtually invisible in the night. The Edhrine guided them with sorcery and, well, just good night vision. Soon enough, he noticed a civilian transport approaching. It was time to see how the Verdarites treated outsiders. The transport ship didn't make it far before a stone from the massive Verdarite warship turned it to dust. Several of the smaller Verdarite ships went in and captured the survivors. The Edhrine knew the Verdarites would do the same to him. He would need a good plan to get in there, if that was even what he wanted anymore. He wondered where the Sentinels were. He wanted to destroy them. He was thinking about this when he realized his ship was on fire.

Stones from the Verdarite warships flew through the air, and men were screaming. The Edhrine turned around and saw one of his men holding a javelin. A second later, the man threw it at Tim. The Edhrine watched as the javelin struck Tim. Tim was dead, and the Edhrine guessed that he wasn't the only one. The Edhrine rushed towards the man who killed Tim.

"For the Verdarite Empire!" the traitorous man shouted.

The Edhrine and the man crossed swords, and the Edhrine killed him with a random dagger while they were in a blade lock. The Edhrine then rushed to put out the fire. He ran into the command center. The entire place was ablaze. The Verdarite warships were closing in, and he only found dead bodies. None of his men were in the command center.

The Edhrine hurried down to the oar section. The men there were dead from sword wounds. That Verdarite infiltrator must have been a good fighter. Then, he found some dead bodies that had spear wounds. The Edhrine's men used spears. That means that either there was friendly fire or there were more Verdarite infiltrators. The Edhrine failed to protect his men. He never thought some of his men could be plotting the downfall of the others. He resolved to remember that the next time he built an army, if there was going to be another army.

The Edhrine rushed to the back of the ship and went around some flaming hallways until he found a door. The Edhrine opened the door and cut the ropes on the other side. A one-man escape boat dropped down, no longer connected to the Sentinel warship. The Edhrine boarded and fled, leaving the sinking and burning ruins of his military behind.

12

The Journey

The Edhrine did not tire. He kept rowing toward the Mohraight Graveyard. If he could get there, he could live in the ruins. He would never have a military again, but the Edhrine did not care. The purpose of the military had been to protect its members. The Edhrine was the leader of the military. The military failed, and so did the Edhrine. Even so, the Edhrine had bigger issues than the past, which he could not control. Sure, he failed his men that he had sworn to try to protect. He never said anything about 100% certainty. He did his best, and therefore, never broke his oath. The Edhrine could live with that.

While rowing, he thought about the Mokror's island and quickly realized there was nowhere to go from there. The Mokror only had rafts, and rowing one of those was not too different from rowing the boat he was in now. The seas were turbulent, and he already capsized four times, but he was still going. The boat had a bucket in it, so he simply had to tip the boat back over, get back in the boat, and then spend time emptying the water. Waves and currents of the Mohraight River weren't a problem when you were in a massive warship.

They certainly were when inside of a one-person boat.

After a few days, the Edhrine made it to the Mohraight Graveyard. The tall spires of rocks towered high above the waterline. It served as a severe danger to large warship, though they did make the water less turbulent. They certainly weren't ideal for keeping one-person boats out. Of course, no sane person would take a one-person boat that far from any known civilized nation, but the Edhrine was not a human nor easily deterred. He began to understand the Mokror's lack of a navy. She didn't need a navy when she had these rocks to defend her. No large warship could hope to get through there.

The Edhrine realized that he needed a place to stop. The Mokror's island was devoid of resources. The Verdarites controlled Mohraight. Sorwond was way too far for the Edhrine to row. The currents of the Mohraight River were usually circular. The Edhrine would be stuck in the ocean for eternity, until he eventually drowned. He couldn't risk the journey to Sorwond. Still, where else could he go? The Edhrine thought about the Sentinel forts north of the Edhormond Mountains. They were further north than Sorwond, but there was land that was much closer to him that connected to the Sentinel forts. The forts were loaded with supplies, and the Edhrine only had to risk drowning for a few days before he got to the Edhormond Mountains. Since Errorunsai did not require food, sleep, or rest, the Edhrine could walk to the Sentinel forts.

The Edhrine could do it, but he felt that he needed to do something more productive than simply rowing. He rowed to the Edhormond Mountains, and since he learned to avoid the obvious signs of currents and large waves, the Edhrine had little to worry about for the day. The waves were not too strong, and the Edhrine was getting a welcome break. Well, it was welcome until it got too long. The Edhrine wanted something other than him rowing to happen. There were not many productive things to do in a one-person boat, but the Edhrine could think of one. He decided to practice his sorcery. It was difficult to use sorcery while trying to row, but not too difficult. He could use his powers in the middle of a battle, after all. He used telekinesis to create small currents. At first, he needed to put his hand in the water, but soon, he began to be able to create smaller currents without touching the water. The Edhrine continued practicing.

Within a few days, the Edhrine could see the Edhormond Mountains. He used sorcery to create a current to give him a speed boost. The Edhrine was exhausted. He was not physically exhausted, because Errorunsai were incapable of becoming exhausted physically. He was exhausted by his near-constant use of sorcery. It was a limit that could be raised by using sorcery more. The Edhrine continued using it despite the urge to just row. He knew that if he didn't hurry, a distant wave would catch up to him and knock him off course. If he got too exhausted, he could lose consciousness and wind up in the circular current. He used that knowledge to drive himself forward, using sorcery to move toward the distant mountains.

The Edhrine drove his boat straight into a jagged rock on the shore. He didn't care that he couldn't go back to sea. If he was done with his journey on the Mohraight River, he was satisfied. He looked around. The entire area was barren, except for rocks and mountains. The Edhrine looked up at the tall mountains. The tops were sharp, and nothing could be built on the extremely steep slopes. There was no building a fortress on the mountain. The Edhrine forgot about that and focused more on how to continue. He used the sun to navigate northward, when he noticed something coming to the shore.

The Edhrine went over to investigate the object. It was large and wooden. The wood appeared to be a fragment of a broken ship. The wood was not scorched, so it couldn't be the Edhrine's ship. He was pretty sure his ship sank anyway. The area was enclosed. It must have been a small closet that never ran into a current. The Edhrine found a door, and he awkwardly opened it and jumped inside. There were dead bodies inside. The Edhrine noticed they were Sentinels. Someone was fighting the Sentinels, and the debris never ran into a current. The Edhrine thought of the possible locations where an item could come to the Edhormond Mountains without hitting a current. The Edhrine deduced that the battle had been further north along the coast. Wait, that meant there were Sentinels in the Sentinel forts he wanted to survive in. That was not good. The Edhrine was a single fighter, and he could not take on the size of the army that would be stationed there. He would have to find a ship and sail to Sorwond, but how would he find one? The only ships in the Sentinel fort area would be Sentinel ships. Or, they could be the people the Sentinels were fighting. The Edhrine would need to sneak past the vigilant Sentinels and then negotiate with a force that could be Verdarite, for all he knew.

The Edhrine would have to survive in the Edhormond Mountains. He could survive, but he would be purposeless. He could just find a place to stay and exist there for the rest of eternity. That was not something the Edhrine could settle with. He wanted to protect people. He thought about the Mokror's alliance. He could join them, but he didn't have an army, and he had nothing to offer. The Edhrine decided the Edhormond

Mountains would do for now. He reminded himself that he didn't have to stay forever.

The Edhrine removed the dead Sentinels from the wreckage and converted it into a usable shelter. He threw the dead Sentinels into the ocean, allowing the waves to constantly push them against the shore. The wreckage had a few holes in it from the rough sea. In the wreckage, he found some random survival equipment. Most of it was useless to him: food, water, and sleeping bags. He did find something of interest, though. He found a pickaxe. He didn't know what he could carve out in the mountains, but over a long time period, he could carve something. It was a minor purpose to exist for, but it was better than absolutely no purpose at all. The Edhrine left his shelter and decided to explore the mountains. If there was a cave near the edge, it might make a better shelter than the wooden wreckage.

The Edhrine encountered something else. He felt something strange every time he looked a certain direction. It was north, towards the Sentinel forts. He knew the Sentinel forts were probably unsafe, but he wanted to follow the feeling. With nothing to lose, the Edhrine went that way. After a while, he noticed that he stopped having the strange feeling when he looked that way. Instead, he felt it when he looked towards the Edhormond Mountains to the west, so he went in that direction. He saw a cave with a strange yellow glow coming from within. He had found something. He was almost certain he knew what it was. It would be a way for him to create an army with sorcery, as his fellow Errorunsai had done. The Mokror created an army of spiders. She made them by connecting the limbs of dead people and animals. Everyone found it disgusting, but that was what she found on the island. The Ifloract manipulated ash and flame. The Edhrine would soon determine how he would make his army. He never particularly wanted an army of sorcery, but that was when he had divisions and divisions of humans. Now, he had a chance to create his own army. He could focus on protecting the rest of the world instead of just his troops.

The Edhrine went into the cave. It was shallow and close to the surface. The Edhrine took ten steps into the cave and encountered a strange altar. The altar was made of an odd dark steel the Edhrine had never seen. It was emitting a glowing, yellow mist. The Edhrine noticed something on top of the altar. It looked like a sword without a blade. It, too, was made of the dark steel. The Edhrine stepped forward and took the sword. When he did, a blade of the glowing, yellow mist formed. The Edhrine tested it against the wall of the cave. The blade was not just solid, but quite sharp. It carved a line into the wall. The Edhrine put the new sword on his hip and left his iron sword and dagger on the altar.

He noticed something else on the altar. There were runes. The Edhrine had never seen them before, but he could understand that they were numbers. Even so, he didn't know what the numbers meant. The numbers were six, four, three, and zero. The Edhrine decided that he probably wouldn't be able to decipher them anytime soon.

The Edhrine also found a book with a cover made of black leather. The Edhrine opened the book. It did not have any evidence of the author, and, like the numbers, was written in a language the Edhrine had never seen but somehow understood. The book detailed how to create an army, how to create the dark steel called Edhormond steel, and how to cut through the stone of the Edhormond Mountains. The Edhrine did not find evidence of any previous civilizations being here. Where did the altar come from? The Edhrine decided to leave the altar alone. He could come back whenever he wanted to practice sorcery.

He immediately began to think about how the Sentinels could be eliminated. The Edhrine knew he was not the only person that they had attacked. The Sentinels attacked countless other small groups and raided them for their own benefit. That was how ancient barbarian groups used to act. The Sentinels would be the first to experience the wrath of the Edhrine's new army.

First, he needed to make the army. The Edhrine decided that his first soldier would be carved out of stone from the cave. He would give the first soldier the honor. He worked for hours, using his new sword to carve out a block of stone. He could have used his crude pickaxe, but that would have taken weeks. The sword was not a mining tool, but its sharp blade would do. The Edhrine carved out the shape of a humanoid. He added eyes, which were two small slits carved with the tip of the Edhrine's sword, to allow the soldier to see. He added ears, which were two slits like the eyes but on the side of the head. The Edhrine stepped back to examine the statue. It had barely any detail; just the basic outline of a human. Still, the Edhrine didn't need anything more. He took the statue and stood it on top of the altar in the cave. The Edhrine focused for a few minutes. When he opened his eyes, he could see the altar had emitted yellow mist, and the statue had stepped off the altar. It remained silent. The Edhrine motioned to the entrance of the cave, and his new soldier walked ahead of him. The Edhrine went back to the wooden wreckage.

The Edhrine pointed to a rock formation nearby. "Over time, we will chisel this into as many humanoid statues as possible. They will be identical to you," the Edhrine announced.

The Edhrine would use his sword when carving, but he did not want to start at that time. He decided to let his soldier do the work for him and go on a scouting mission. Informing the soldier that he would be gone, he ordered it to continue laboring at its task. The Edhrine told it to attack any Verdarites or Sentinels, but anyone else could come up to it. It was not sure how it knew what a Verdarite or Sentinel is, but the soldier nodded its head. The Edhrine went north.

The soldier chiseled away at the rock. It did not feel anything other than the need to chisel the rock. Its creator had ordered it to do that, so that is what it would do. In the meantime, it wondered what a Verdarite or Sentinel was. It was not worried because a Verdarite or Sentinel would not be able to connect it to its creator. The soldier would do its job, and chisel away at the rock, making statue copies of itself. As the soldier continued to chisel away at the rock, it wondered what its creator was called. It knew that he was not simply "the creator." It knew he had a name. The soldier continued chiseling and did not notice when its creator came up behind it.

"I am impressed. You chiseled out two statues of yourself while I was gone. Come over here," the Edhrine ordered.

The soldier followed. The Edhrine wanted to offer the soldier a break, but the Edhrine knew better. First, the soldier probably couldn't feel appreciation. Second, the soldier never got tired or bored, so he wouldn't even want a break. The Edhrine realized he just referred to a stone statue as he. The Edhrine figured that the statue was technically a living thing.

The Edhrine and the soldier stopped at the wooden wreckage. The Edhrine showed the soldier a log. "I need you to turn this into a better tools, so you can work more efficiently," he ordered, "I will use my sword to chisel with you."

The soldier was crafting a pickaxe of wood when it noticed something approaching. A small ship approached. It was not a one-person boat. Rather, it was big enough for one bunk room and a small room for oars. It seemed to be a patrol craft. The soldier informed its creator.

The Edhrine said to the soldier, "Let us greet them."

The Edhrine and his creation walked to the stone beach. The boat dropped a small anchor not far from the shore and a man rowed a small raft to the Edhrine. He got off the raft and walked up to him. His first reaction was to inquire about the stone statue.

"What is that?" the mysterious man asked.

The Edhrine answered, "He is a soldier."

The soldier took note of that. The Edhrine thought of him as a person. He would do the same.

"Okay, then," the man replied. "Then who are you?"

"I would like to know if you are aligned with any faction before I answer."

"Okay, I am independent. I've been bringing people from wherever they were to wherever they wanted to go. I'll be honest, I've transported all sorts of people, some of which were aligned with some of the factions."

"Which factions?" the Edhrine asked.

"I've transported some men loyal to someone called the Edhrine, I've transported some men called Sentinels hunting those men, and then I transported the Edhrine's men once again, and they burned a Sentinel base to the ground."

The Edhrine decided that revealing his real name was unwise when he introduced himself. "I am Edhorm." The Edhrine hoped the man wouldn't notice how he just used a part of the name of the mountain range they were in for a false name.

"Are you stranded here in the Edhormond Mountains? I can take you to a city, for a price."

The Edhrine thought about it. He and his soldier could leave these mountains, and he could start another faction. However, if he left the mountains, he would leave behind the altar and the cave. If some ancient civilization left behind the secret to creating an army, then they could have left more. He couldn't risk missing it. He told the man that he was staying in the Edhormond Mountains.

The mysterious man nodded, and soon left. He sailed along the shore.

The Edhrine figured he was looking for stranded people, hoping to earn some favors. The Edhrine turned to his creation. "We are going to make more of you."

"How will this be done?" the soldier asked.

"I will demonstrate." The Edhrine decided to make his own altar. Only his first soldier would have the honor of being made on top of the altar in the cave, and only he would have the honor of being chiseled from the stone making up the wall in the cave.

The soldier followed the Edhrine to a random point near the cave. The Edhrine and the soldier chiseled a portion of the mountains out, making a slab of stone. The Edhrine figured it would do. He went toward the slab and placed the two statues that the first soldier chiseled out on it. The Edhrine then stepped back and focused. He verbally commanded the altar to bring the statues to life once he saw it start leaking yellow mist. Not long after, the statues moved. They were his next soldiers. The new soldiers stepped forward and wordlessly followed the Edhrine back to the makeshift shelter in the wooden wreckage. There, the Edhrine told them all to chisel at the mountains. He would be getting plenty of soldiers, and he would eliminate the

Sentinels and stop their relentless conquests of the world. The Sentinels would have big issues when the Edhrine showed up with his new army.

13

The Fortress

The Edhrine and his three soldiers walked to a random part of the mountain, not far from the wooden wreckage. The Edhrine gave each some crude chiseling tools. It would take time, but the Edhrine and his new soldiers were immune to boredom. Boredom, if it could even be called that, only struck when there was a lack of anything productive to do. So long as a task was productive, neither the Edhrine nor his men would have an issue with it. The Edhrine's purpose had been in jeopardy when he was at risk of being eternally stranded. Now, he knew what he was going to do, and he informed his soldiers as well. They worked for days without breaking. The soldiers chiseled stone blocks, and the Edhrine transformed the blocks into statues. Periodically, the Edhrine went to the stone slab he made and used it as an altar to turn the statues into men. Every day, the army grew. New soldiers would go north and get trees, and the Edhrine would occasionally take a break from chiseling to turn the wood into something that resembled a chisel. In this way, the army grew. The process was slow, but certain. The army grew faster with assistance of every new soldier.

The Edhrine knew he could not remain at the Edhormond Mountains forever. Eventually, some civilization would try to come to the Edhormond Mountains and settle there. He couldn't have that. The Edhrine would need to secure the land and publicly declare himself. After all, only an idiot would try to settle on the front lawn of a powerful army. He needed to figure out how to get some actual weapons. Few would be intimidated by an army of soldiers with no armor and wooden chisels for weapons. The Sentinels would come and crush his army and repeat what happened at Mohraight all over again. The Edhrine didn't want to have to find a third army. He needed to make forges, and produce the Edhormond steel that the book mentioned. The Edhormond steel was very strong, and between that and an army, the Edhrine would be unstoppable. It would only be a matter of time.

Still, an army without a base was not going to do. The Edhrine needed a place for these forges, and it needed to be well-defended. If the Edhrine didn't protect his forges, someone would come along and use the Edhormond steel for their own armies. That was one of the last things the Edhrine needed. However, there were no defensive structures of any kind in the Edhormond Mountains. The only two things that didn't seem natural were the strange altar and the wooden wreckage. Neither of those would protect anything. Since there was nothing to occupy, that left the harder option: to build a fortress himself. He would need better tools, so the first forge would be defenseless. It wouldn't be a problem. The Edhrine would destroy the forge once he crafted enough tools to make something defensible. He could create new forges inside of a fortress anyway.

The Edhrine ordered his soldiers to begin carving stones into bricks. With those bricks, he built a small furnace. It would do. The Edhrine created a fire rune inside the bottom chamber. He created a chamber above the fire chamber for the actual Edhormond steel. The steel would be molten and cast into whatever it was to become.

Next, the Edhrine instructed his soldiers to collect the darker-colored rocks in the mountains. The Edhrine knew they were a strange type of living crystal. It wasn't the first strange sorcery-related thing he discovered. At that point, the Edhrine was hardly surprised. The crystal itself was nearly immune to heat. However, when heated to the right temperature, pockets of Edhormond steel within the crystal became molten and flowed out. The Edhormond steel could be produced without limit, although it would take time. Just like wood could be infinitely produced by planting trees, Edhormond steel could be farmed by growing it in the crystals. The crystals easily survived when floating in water, so the Edhrine could let them grow Edhormond steel in a tub of water before taking them to the forges to extract the Edhormond steel.

The only problem with this grand plan was that the crystals weren't exactly common. The soldiers had to venture deep within caves or ravines to find some growing in a rare pool of water. They would separate the crystals from the stone and carry them back to the Edhrine. The Edhrine readied a few tubs of water. The soldiers transferred the almost-dead crystals to the water tubs. Soon, they grew trace amounts of Edhormond steel. The dark crystals were visibly showing black growths on the outside and some of the holes traversing them filled with the material. That black material was Edhormond steel.

Once there existed a satisfactory amount of Edhormond steel, the Edhrine brought his collection of crystals to the forge. He watched as the black material became a glowing yellow fluid. The molten metal flowed out of the crystals, forming a small puddle of molten Edhormond steel in the forge. Some soldiers brought the crystals back to the water pools as other soldiers drained the forge using stone buckets. They were heavy, but the Edhrine wasn't about to try to hold the molten metal with buckets made of heat-conducting iron, or even worse, wood. The soldiers poured the contents into stone casts. They were essentially rods of varying length. The longest one was for pikes, the second-longest for spears, and the shortest for swords or daggers. These rods could also be repurposed for chisels and pickaxes. The only cast that was not a rod was a rectangular cast, which was for shields. The weapon casts all lacked heads because the Edhrine had other ideas for the heads.

The Edhrine took several newly made rods and brought them to the altar in the cave. He placed a medium-sized rod onto the table. "Altar, make these weapons of steel and mist."

"Very well," a voice replied from the altar.

A yellow mist enshrouded the altar. The Edhrine remained still and silent until it parted. Where the head of the newly created pickaxe should have been was a pickaxe head of yellow mist. The Edhrine took it to the mountainside and swung it into the stone with all his strength. The stone cracked, small chunks of stone flying in all directions. The pickaxe head was completely unscathed. The yellow mist moved around but maintained its shape. It was always easy to see just how sharp the ends of the pickaxe head were. The Edhrine guessed they could put a hole in iron armor if swung with enough force. He could only imagine the kind of damage such a blade could do if put on a spear. The Edhrine's army would be difficult to defeat with such sharp weapons and strong armor. Sure, the armor was not invincible, but the Edhrine didn't need it to be. He needed it to look intimidating because the Edhrine never underestimated the value of psychological warfare. Also, the armor needed to be strong enough for a foot soldier. Armor made of a thin layer of Edhormond steel met both criteria.

The Edhrine made gear for himself as well. His gear consisted of thicker layers of Edhormond steel, since being an Errorunsai made him slightly stronger than his soldiers. The Edhrine decided he would make his own gear first. With the first Edhormond steel pickaxe, he went to some stone that his soldiers chiseled out. Rather than making it into his next soldier, he made the stone into casts for his armor. He knew his armor would be different from that of his men. Therefore, these casts would likely only be used once. He went to the forges and used the heavy stone buckets to dump molten Edhormond steel into the casts. He waited for the steel to cool and then removed the armor pieces. The Edhrine returned to the cave with the altar to change into his new gear. After all, he had never shown anyone his face, and he didn't intend to change that.

The Edhrine marched back to his men. At first, they didn't recognize him, but they let him in because of the Edhormond steel gear. When the Edhrine told them his name, they realized that this was not a special visitor and got back to work.

The Edhrine then made casts for his soldiers' armor. With that, he was finished. All the armor and weapons were finished. The Edhrine now could focus on his fortress. He had tools and more. It was time to start building.

The Edhrine told his soldiers to stop chiseling away at the mountainside. He brought his troops to a specific place. It was a cliff face. There was also a bulge further north, where the Edhrine instructed his men to mine. He envisioned a thin passageway and a huge gate at the cliff face. Building this fortress would take years, but the Edhrine had patience. He knew his purpose and the purpose of the fortress. That drove away any trace of boredom. The Edhrine directed his soldiers, pointing out how tall the passageways should be and the direction it should go. His plan was to connect the huge gate to a maze with a staircase leading to the actual fortress above. The entryway in the bulge in the mountainside would be a direct route to the fortress that bypassed the maze. The fortress would be underground, and the important rooms would be nearly invulnerable to catapults. Sure, the top rooms would be gone, but the attacker needed two things: knowledge of the location of the upper rooms and lots and lots of patience.

The Edhrine's soldiers chiseled away at stone for two years before they finally completed. The Edhrine constructed rooms for mining stone and sculpting it into soldiers. He built a room with a large altar for turning the mass-produced statues into soldiers. He made a room for the unarmed statues to stand, waiting for the next initiation session. He created an armory for the Edhormond steel weapons. He planned for a room for initiation. It was something he would need to do to all of his soldiers. Previously, the Edhrine initiated the soldiers manually, one by one. However, if they reached a soldier production rate as high as he wanted, the Edhrine would no longer be able to initiate them individually. He would need to mass-initiate them just like he mass-produced them. That room would have to wait, though, since he didn't really need to dig out a pit for mass-initiation at this time. He could do individual initiations for now.

The Edhrine initiated the last soldier for the day and then walked into the quarters he constructed for himself. There was a window, one of the few in the fortress, and an altar. The door could be locked, so he could remove his armor undisturbed without anyone seeing him. Still, the Edhrine had little reason to remove his armor. He probably wouldn't use the lock often. The window had a stone platform in front of it, on which the Edhrine could stand when he looked out. The Edhrine's view was nothing special in the Edhormond Mountains. It simply looked at other mountains in the range. You could get the same view by merely climbing a mountain. Either way, the two years of work paid off. The huge Edhormond steel gate was installed at the front of the maze, as was a stone door for the entrance that bypassed the maze. The stone door blended in with the mountainside. For extra defense, the back of the door was plated with Edhormond steel. If someone busted through the solid rock, there was a false tomb behind that would deter anyone who stumbled into it by accident. Still, nobody mines into a secret chamber by accident, especially when the secret chamber is next to a big, suspicious Edhormond steel gate. Behind the false tomb and through another reinforced secret door was the staircase into the fortress. It led into a random hallway, which lead into the depths of the fortress.

The Edhrine decided that there were enough soldiers. He had a fortress, forges, and twenty-five crystals producing Edhormond steel. There was little else he needed. It was time to hunt the Sentinels. Their raids on innocent would be over. Finally, people would be safe from the far-reaching and elusive armies. The Edhrine's seven divisions would crush them. The Edhrine's soldiers were better equipped and more numerous than the Sentinels. This was the end for all that had ever marched under the banner of the Sentinels.

14

The Hunt

Verdar VI looked down at the man before him, Admiral I. Verdar VI had already tried an experienced admiral and then a new one with an elite prototype. He finally defeated the Edhrine when he sent his best: Admiral I. Admiral I was going to receive a lot of medals for the victory at Mohraight against the Edhrine. Next, Admiral I would be going to Nacreato. Mohraight had fallen, and Nacreato, the enemy of Mohraight, was next.

Across the world from Verdar and his admiral, the Edhrine and his men marched north to the Sentinel forts. After a long march, they could see the fort compound. The Edhrine told his men to ready their spears. The Edhrine's soldiers were in a phalanx, and they all had shields. No arrow would reach any of them. When a volley of arrows launched from a Sentinels fort, the Edhrine's phalanx turned and marched in that direction. The Edhrine, in the back of the phalanx, watched as his men reached the gate. The Edhrine signaled for them to part, and he marched forward. A Sentinel stood on the top of the gate.

"Who are you and what do you want?" the Sentinel asked.

"Who are you and why did you attack me unprovoked?" the

Edhrine countered.

"We thought you were attacking. Look, nobody died. Is there an issue?" the Sentinel replied.

"Yes, there is. The Sentinels are murderers. I have lost count of how many villages you have massacred," the Edhrine denounced.

"Kill them!" the Sentinel shouted.

"That is exactly what I am referring to," the Edhrine snickered.

The Edhrine's soldiers put their shields up and blocked the arrows. It wasn't long before the Edhrine snuck around to the back of the fort and climbed in. He reached the men on the wall and sent them flying over the wall, into the forest of spears that was the phalanx of living statues. The Edhrine's soldiers removed the fallen Sentinels from the ends of their spears as the Edhrine opened the gate for them.

After a search of the fort, they found more dead Sentinels than they could count. The Edhrine definitely didn't kill those. Someone else had fought them and won. It wasn't long before he found the first evidence of who. A spider lay on the ground, speared by a fallen Sentinel. In another hallway, an ashen body holding a long halberd lay dead with an arrow to the faceplate. The Mokror and the Ifloract tried to eliminate the Sentinel presence to convince the Edhrine to join their anti-Verdarite alliance.

The Edhrine figured that there were more Sentinels than the ones his fellow Errorunsai killed. He would need to hunt the Sentinels, and he would find them, once he got a navy. When you have an army, it doesn't help when it's stuck on a continent that isn't connected to any major civilizations. The Edhrine, of course, had a plan for that. He went to the harbor in the Sentinel forts. It was the hidden one that the Sentinels used to escape. The Edhrine guessed that the Mokror and Ifloract didn't know about the harbor. He was right. There were not only five Sentinel ships, but also an army of Sentinels marching onto them. The Edhrine and his soldiers rushed in and tried to capture as many ships as they could.

Deciding to go personally for the closest ship, the Edhrine ran up its ramp with two soldiers trailing behind him. There was a single Sentinel standing at the top of the ramp. The Sentinel threw a dagger, which the Edhrine caught and sent it flying back into the Sentinel's face. Grabbing the fallen Sentinel, the Edhrine threw him off the ramp to avoid blocking the soldiers marching up the ramp behind him. The Edhrine jumped onto a crate and found three Sentinels taking cover behind it, while shooting arrows at the soldiers coming up the ramp. The Edhrine sent them tumbling over the railing and into the water below. He didn't waste time checking on their status. Rather, he rushed into the captain's quarters and found the Sentinel captain and two bodyguards.

"I do not have time for this," the Edhrine informed them.

"Go! Go! Go!" one of the bodyguards yelled.

The captain ran, and the bodyguards took defensive stances. The Edhrine did not have time for a fight. He dodged the first bodyguard's spear thrust and then charged at the second, killing him. He ran after the captain, leaving the first bodyguard alive.

Meanwhile, the Edhrine's first soldier dueled another Sentinel captain. His creator had ordered them to fight, so that was what the soldiers were doing. He parried the Sentinel captain's sword strike with the shaft of his spear and quickly impaled the man with the spearhead. Removing the spear from the captain's body, the soldier left the captain's quarters to find the rest of the Sentinels.

Still chasing his target, the Edhrine found that the captain was already in a one-man boat, attempting to row out of the harbor. Running and jumping, the Edhrine was on top of the boat in a few seconds. The boat flipped over, rendering the captain defenseless. The Edhrine dragged the captain out of the water and went back to his army. The soldiers stood in a grid formation. Several Sentinel prisoners were lined up in front of them. The Edhrine shoved the captain alongside the other captured Sentinels.

"You have all done well," the Edhrine commended his army.

Only one of the Sentinel ships escaped, since it was on the far side of the harbor.

The Edhrine then turned to the prisoners. "I want information," the Edhrine demanded.

The prisoners remained silent.

The Edhrine pressed, "Tell me where to find some more Sentinels."

The prisoners kept their mouths shut.

"Silence will not be of value anyone. You are going to go to the Verdarites at Mohraight. We will leave you there and you will hope that the Verdarites do not decide to kill you on sight."

The Edhrine's empty threat still didn't persuade them to speak.

"It may help you to know that I can find out your whereabouts from some friends of mine. Speak and save everyone's time. Or, as I said, the Verdarites will get you to reveal the whereabouts of your comrades."

The prisoners still remained silent.

"Very well. Put them on a ship and send them to the Mokror's island."

A prisoner finally spoke, "What happened to the threat about the Verdarites at Mohraight?"

The Edhrine answered, "I am not that barbaric."

"Who is the Mokror?" asked another prisoner.

The Edhrine continued, "Honestly, I do not know if she would be worse than the Verdarites. She will definitely not kill you, but you are not going to be fond of the living conditions…or the guards."

The Edhrine knew they wouldn't want to be locked in a spider-infested sewer system. He watched as his soldiers loaded the prisoners onto a ship. The Edhrine's entire fleet set sail for the Mokror's island.

When they arrived, the Edhrine's soldiers marched the prisoners off the ships and the Edhrine went to speak with the Mokror.

"What brings you to my island?" the Mokror inquired.

The Edhrine answered, "I have a few prisoners for you that I do not need. I see you went to war with the Sentinels in hopes of recruiting me?"

"You are correct," the Mokror acknowledged.

"Your strike on the Sentinels is appreciated, but it did not eliminate them. The Sentinels are still at large, spreading evil across the world."

The Mokror continued to make her case. "If you join us, the Sentinels will perish when they're stuck between us and the Verdarites. They'll be stuck in no man's land between murderous Verdarites and us."

The Edhrine explained, "The Sentinels are still able to cause harm. They need to be fully eliminated before the Verdarites are an issue."

"You've seen what the Verdarites have. They want you to do this. They are going to sit back and watch you lose troops to the Sentinels and then come and finish you off."

"I have better ways of getting troops now," the Edhrine told her. Clearly, the Mokror hadn't yet realized that the men under the dark armor were not humans. She probably thought the Edhrine had just gotten some new armor. "Those men are not men. They are stone brought to life. They are from the Edhormond Mountains."

"So, you finally switched to an army of sorcery? What happened to the humans?" the Mokror questioned.

"They were all killed at Mohraight by Verdarite infiltrators. I rowed a single-person boat to the Edhormond Mountains and found an altar for sorcery. It is a long story, but now I have a functional army."

"You were always resourceful. But why didn't you come to my island?"

"I could offer nothing to your alliance, not having an army. There are few resources on this island. I had nothing to do here, so I made the journey to the Edhormond Mountains. I planned to go to the Sentinel forts, but I saw ships there and decided that they might be Verdarites and therefore the forts were not an option. Obviously, those were your ships. I ended up making an army in the Edhormond Mountains."

"You have a lot to bring to the table even without your new legions of stone soldiers. Your tactical skill is getting well-known. We captured some Sentinel letters that were making their way to Sentinel ships. They were in the wrong place at the wrong time, and we seized them. It seems plenty of soldiers that are not supposed to be hunting you knew about you. Normally, the Sentinels only tell their soldiers who the target is, and nobody else. The letters contained warnings saying to avoid a battle if they saw you, because of your tactics."

"I am glad to know I have a reputation among them, but that hardly gives me an advantage. If anything, it raises the chance of Sentinels surviving a battle."

"What about the Verdarites? Do you think you don't have a reputation with them? We didn't intercept letters from them, but it isn't hard to guess that they would know about your exploits. I know that you commanded a Verdarite warship for a time using disguises. I learned additional details from the intercepted Sentinel letters."

"It seems that the Sentinels need to better secure their letters," the Edhrine chuckled, ignoring the obvious attempt to recruit him to the anti-Verdarite alliance.

"Indeed," the Mokror replied.

"What I need are positions of the Sentinels. If I am going to eliminate them, I need to know where they went."

"I can't help you. We intercepted the letters weeks ago, and since then we haven't detected any Sentinel activity. They've gone into hiding."

"How inconvenient. I will need to find them."

15

The Alliance

The Edhrine returned to the Edhormond Mountains. He searched for the Sentinels to no avail. More and more, he thought about the Verdarites. The Sentinels would remain a grave threat to everybody, but if the Sentinels were unavailable, then he would have to switch to the Verdarites. Besides, if the Sentinels were hiding, they weren't oppressing innocent civilians. Therefore, the Edhrine could focus his attention elsewhere. He made the decision to go back to the Mokror's island.

Some time later, the Edhrine's first soldier stood at the front of the ship. He gazed into the horizon, like the rest of the soldiers in the phalanx behind him. The Edhrine was returning to the strange island, and none of the soldiers knew quite why.

After a few days journey, the Edhrine lowered the ramps onto the Mokror's Island and ordered his troops to march down. The Edhrine went ahead of the phalanx, to meet the Mokror and the Ifloract who were waiting below.

"Back so soon?" the Mokror asked.

The Ifloract asked, "What is he doing here?"

Despite being enemies from a long time ago, the Edhrine and the Ifloract didn't try to kill each other. That alone was impressive, and they were about to enter an unprecedented alliance.

The Edhrine announced, "I am here to join your anti-Verdarite alliance. The Sentinels went into hiding, and are therefore not a threat I can deal with. Most likely, they are not a threat to anyone."

The Mokror responded, "We were looking forward to this moment. The Verdarites are growing powerful, and we need help to keep them out of Sorwond. They are beginning to overrun the South Morhor Mountains and from there they will be at the Depths of Flame soon."

"My base is quite vulnerable to flooding. We have reason to believe large quantities of water are moving through the mountains as we speak. We need to recapture those mountains if you want to keep me on your side," the Ifloract declared.

"The Depths of Flame are of utmost importance if we plan on using your living flames. They will be quite effective at burning enemy siege engines," pointed out the Edhrine.

"We could burn the wagons before they reach my base, halting the entire attempt. From there, we can recapture the South Morhor Mountains and free the civilians who live in the caves. The civilians we free will fight on our side, so this will increase our numbers," the Ifloract said.

"How many people have you liberated from Verdarites so far?" the Edhrine questioned.

The Mokror answered, "None. All of the areas the Verdarites captured have remained firmly in their grasp."

"Then how do you know civilians will join us if you never liberated any?" the Edhrine asked.

The Ifloract responded, "That's what happens in every other war against an evil power. It's what we've been doing for the last millennium while you were working on your little faction."

"Move troops out of the South Morhor Mountains," the Edhrine instructed.

"What?" both the Mokror and the Ifloract asked in unison.

"If we move troops out of the South Morhor Mountains, the enemy will take the entire thing, but they will press on to the Depths of Flame if they know who the Ifloract is. This will draw them out into the open plain, where the Ifloract's long halberds have the advantage. The living flames will burn the wagons that are full of water," the Edhrine explained.

The Ifloract questioned, "Are you trying to get me killed?"

"If I wanted to kill you, I would have done it right here and now with my sword," the Edhrine informed him calmly.

"Enough. We need to kill the Verdarites, not each other," the Mokror said.

The Edhrine, Mokror, and Ifloract discussed the approach they would execute. The Ifloract opposed the Edhrine's original plan, so the Mokror also refused to go along with it. The Edhrine then presented another idea. He said that the troops would position themselves within the civilian caves, and they would slowly kill off the Verdarites when they took over. The Ifloract's base would be safe.

A week later, the Edhrine was in a cave with a legion of his stone soldiers. They were fully armed and deadly. The Edhrine's first soldier quickly became more important than the others. He had different armor, which better suited recon missions. The Edhrine already sent him on five missions to determine the Verdarites' plans. His impressive ability to stalk enemies undetected earned him the unique set of armor and the place as the Edhrine's second-in-command.

The Edhrine reviewed his maps as he listened to the sound of the Verdarites marching. As far as he was aware, the Verdarites were on the march into the South Morhor Mountains. As previously instructed by the Edhrine, the natives offered no resistance. They peacefully remained in their caves, allowing the Verdarite forces to pass. The Edhrine knew the Verdarites would secure the area and make sure that no armies were present before they began searching civilian areas and massacring natives. The Verdarites marched along the many mountain roads, their spears pointed forward.

After an hour of searching, the Verdarites moved towards the caves. If the Verdarites could search the South Morhor Mountains in one hour, they must have had a lot of troops. Either way, the Edhrine went to the entrance of the cave and told the guards to move away. The guards went down into the cave, and the Edhrine removed his helmet. He blew into a horn, signaling the other members of the alliance to strike. The Edhrine put his helmet back on and listened to two other horns blowing in the distance, repeating the signal to the troops too far to hear the first horn. The Edhrine watched as confused Verdarite soldiers broke formation and pointed their spears outward. A few backed into caves. The Edhrine chuckled to himself, and watched as spearmen rushed out of the cave the Verdarites were backing into and impaled them. He turned his attention to other Verdarite groups, noticing similar results.

The Ifloract hovered over his men who were marching out of a cave. His men needed the largest caves because of their long polearms. The Ifloract would have plenty of room to relax once his armies were out.

"Go, find some Verdarites for us to kill," the Ifloract told some living flames.

The flames wordlessly hovered out of the cave entrance. The Ifloract then levitated out himself, taking position above the long halberds of his army. He looked below as the ashen soldiers pointed their halberds forward and attacked Verdarite armies. On another mountain, the Ifloract saw the Mokror's spiders on the sides of cliffs jumping onto Verdarite squads, and the Edhrine's new soldiers marching in formation to engage the Verdarite armies in phalanx-to-phalanx combat. The Errorunsai's troops were winning.

On a nearby cliff, Verdar VI was overlooking the battle. The legion he had sent to scout the mountains had drawn the enemy forces out. Six of Verdar VI's legions surrounded the area. After the advance scout legion fell, the enemy would find themselves surrounded. As the emperor of the Verdarites, he knew what he was doing. He was fighting the Ifloract, master of fire with legions of the world's longest polearms, the Mokror, a commander of filthy spiders capable of unusual maneuvers, and, most recently, a new enemy. The new enemy was clad in black steel, commanding soldiers with similar armor. Verdar VI was not quite sure who this new enemy was, but it did not matter. The new enemy would die with the old ones.

"Send in legions one through six. Inform them that legion seven was defeated, and it is their time to avenge the fallen," Verdar VI ordered.

The Edhrine heard marching and looked around. All he saw were dead bodies and his soldiers who were still alive. He had nine divisions left, which was plenty considering he had come with only one more than that. Still, the approaching marching was loud. Whoever it was brought a lot of soldiers. The Edhrine walked into a cave and was met by his second-in-command.

"Creator, there are six legions of Verdarites surrounding our current position. They are closing in. The first legion they sent to us acted as a diversion, intended to draw us out. We do not have enough time to return to the caves," the second-in-command explained.

"This is problematic," the Edhrine said. "Have the Ifloract order his living flames to light the ground on fire around us. Leave no way in or out. We do not require food. We can handle an indefinite siege."

Verdar VI looked on. He saw the floating flames, the living flames of the Ifloract, come forth from the area where the enemies were. What were they planning? Suddenly, they began pummeling the ground below them with fiery projectiles. Verdar VI understood right away. They surrounded themselves with a circle of flame, which the Verdarites would not be able to pass. The circle of flame did not appear to be burning out. That was something Verdar VI needed to remember. They could make fire that lack of fuel did not extinguish.

The Edhrine looked at the flaming barrier that protected them. He saw the Verdarite armies on the other side, standing in formation. The Edhrine motioned for one of his soldiers to grab a bow. The bow was shaped like a square bracket, with a string of glowing yellow mist. The bow limbs were made of Edhormond steel. Like the other Edhormond steel weapons, the bow was forged when the Edhrine first found the Edhormond steel-growing crystals. The arrows had shafts of Edhormond steel and heads of yellow mist, as could be expected of an Edhormond weapon.

"Fire!" the Edhrine ordered. Several arrows escaped through the flames. The Edhrine heard screams. It worked.

The Edhrine told the Ifloract his plan of attack. "I will order my archers to fire through the flames at the Verdarites. Your living flames will do the same from above. The Verdarites will be unable to return fire."

Verdar VI ordered the legions to pull back. The enemy forces were shooting arrows and flaming projectiles through their circle of fire, and Verdar VI was not about to let them destroy his entire army that way. He ordered the archers to the front, in order to shoot back. The Verdarite archers were far more numerous than anything the enemies could bring. He also ordered wagons to get water from the nearest river. It would be over for the enemies.

The Edhrine saw the Verdarite legions moving backwards and predicted that the Verdarite commander, whoever he was, would bring his archers forward. The Edhrine stood safely behind a rock with his archers as the Verdarite arrow rain hit nothing but dirt. The Edhrine just needed to determine the enemy tactician's next move.

Verdar VI looked on as the wagons of water advanced. The archers had not yet stopped firing, and Verdar VI imagined his enemies dying by the hundreds in the rain of arrows. He knew, however, that they probably took cover when the legions started moving, instead of continuing to fire. Verdar VI knew, then, that the water wagons would go undetected, since the enemies would not dare peak above their cover.

The Edhrine heard water, and he heard a lot of it. He did not look over the rock. The arrows were still firing. He did, however, now hear the sounds of the Verdarite legions moving forward again. The Edhrine knew what they did.

"To the caves!" the Edhrine shouted to his men. Sure, the Verdarites were still raining arrows on them, but they had much better odds of surviving a run through the arrow rain than they did surviving melee combat with the legions. The Edhrine's soldiers held bows, and they would not be able to survive melee combat for very long.

The Ifloract peered out the entryway to the cave he was in. He saw the Edhrine walking calmly to the entrance with his archers.

"The Verdarites brought water to destroy the perimeter. They are on the march. We will use this cave entrance as a choke point. They will fall to the rain of fire and arrows I will prepare. This cave has no other entrances. The Verdarites will have to leave or die," the Edhrine explained.

"I will order my living flames to get ready," the Ifloract replied.

The Edhrine walked past the Ifloract into the deeper parts of the cave system. They were lucky to find a cave with only one entrance, which contained enough room for a large number of troops. The Edhrine would be able to last a long time in the caves, and the Verdarites would have to find another way through.

Verdar VI stood on a mountain across from the cave that his enemies entered. The enemy with the black steel armor appeared to be the one giving orders. Verdar VI assumed the new enemy was brought in to be a tactician, and he was a good one. That enemy tactician almost seemed familiar, though. Verdar VI turned and looked into the distant cave. He could barely see some of the long halberds of the Ifloract's soldiers pointing toward the entrance. Verdar VI knew what to do.

The Edhrine heard clashing of weapons at the cave entrance. The Verdarites took the bait. When the Edhrine came to the cave entryway, he observed six Verdarite swordsmen dead on the floor and the Ifloract's two soldiers still standing guard.

A voice reported, "We defeated them. As predicted, the

Verdarites sent swordsmen to attempt to get around the long halberds."

The Edhrine knew that one of his archers was talking. The Edhrine had set a trap in the cave entryway, hoping to lure Verdarite swordsmen and then kill them with archers hidden behind cover. It worked, and now the Edhrine needed to make sure the enemy didn't catch on to the plot.

It took the Verdarites a long time to figure out what was happening. About twenty-five swordsmen were sent into the cave entryway before the Verdarites realized there was a trap. The Edhrine didn't celebrate, though. The Verdarites had just lost half a division out of their six legions. The Edhrine estimated they had around 2900 or maybe 2800 men left, if the casualties from the Edhrine's archer attack were included. That was still a lot of Verdarites. The Edhrine had nine divisions of his spearmen, and they would not be able to win in open combat yet. The Edhrine needed to lower the Verdarite numbers even more.

Verdar VI looked into the cave and turned to his tactical advisor. "How did you not realize that there were archers in there?"

"I do not know, my emperor. I thought that the swordsmen survived and gone deeper. I could not see the bodies from he—" The tactical advisor was interrupted by Verdar VI's hand shoving him over a cliff.

"Get me a new tactical advisor," Verdar VI ordered one of his bodyguards. Verdar VI then looked at the cave "and bring catapults."

The Edhrine heard chanting outside the cave. He decided to risk peaking.

"Darn it," the Edhrine mumbled.

There were catapults outside, and the Verdarites were chanting some war cry. The catapults could collapse the cave if left unchecked. The Edhrine had to do something.

Verdar VI watched as the catapults pummeled the mountain before him. The enemy forces cowered within the caves, but those caves would be full of stone and gravel soon. The catapults flung stones at the mountain, in strategically selected locations above the cave entrances. The target placement was designed to collapse the caves. Verdar VI was going to win.

The Edhrine ordered some living flames to the cave entrance. Dust blanketed the area as the catapults continued to barrage the cave entrance with boulders. The Edhrine ordered some spearmen to charge outside. He would lose troops from this move, but it was for a good cause. The spearmen would distract the enemy while the living flames destroyed the catapults from above. Some spearmen would die, but the rest would live.

Verdar VI saw some of those dark spearmen rush out of the cave entrance. Verdar VI counted about a division's worth of them.

"Destroy them!" Verdar VI shouted.

The Verdarite legions rushed forth with spears and pikes leveled at the dark spearmen. The spearmen formed a square of outward-facing shields and pointed their spears outward. The spearmen were surrounded.

The living flames floated high above the battlefield. With the entire Verdarite army focused on the spearmen, no one spotted the living flames floating towards the catapults. Floating behind and above the catapults, the living flames released their barrage.

Verdar VI was watching his legions surround the enemy spearmen when he heard the sound of fire. He turned towards the catapults in time to witness a division of living flames open fire on his catapults. The catapults burst into an explosion of flames, killing nearby Verdarites. The living flames retreated to their caves, away from the charred wreckage of the catapults.

The Edhrine signaled the spearmen to return to the cave. They slowly moved their formation towards the cave entrance, losing men fast to the Verdarite army. The Edhrine knew what he would do next. Once the few surviving spearmen returned to the cave, the Edhrine ordered living flames to go out again and make a new flaming barrier. However, this one was not to keep the Verdarites out. Instead, the barrier was to keep the Verdarites in. The Verdarites would be unable to leave and their supplies would be unable to enter. Without catapults, their only method of attack would be to rush the caves. With archers around every corner, the Verdarites would not last long. The Errorunsai would win this fight.

The Ifloract found the Edhrine at the cave entrance. The Edhrine had just ordered the Ifloract's living flames for the second time.

"Have you ordered my troops without my knowledge or permission?" the Ifloract questioned.

The Edhrine responded that he did.

"What were you thinking?" continued the Ifloract.

"I was thinking that we would win the battle, and I was correct." The Edhrine gestured to the Verdarites who were starting to realize the situation that they were in.

The Ifloract snapped, "I do not care about results. Ordering my troops without my permission is not an insult that I take lightly."

"Are you that desperate to start another war?" the Edhrine replied. "You are taking as an insult a move that will give you more credit than you deserve. Any who look at this battle will assume you ordered the living flames. You will get more out of accepting this than starting a war with me. Besides, the Verdarites are threatening enough. You don't want to fight me as well."

"Well, then… let's see who will win the war that will come after the Verdarites."

"Since you are evidently so disappointed with my command of your troops, I will take back my last order."

"Do it!" the Ifloract dared.

The Edhrine was rather disappointed that the Ifloract was starting a war over this. At least he had said that they could remain allies until after the Verdarites were gone. Either way, the Ifloract didn't catch the reason for the Edhrine's last statement. Taking back his last order meant that the Verdarites were free to leave. They would quickly realize they had more valuable targets to attack than the South Morhor Mountains. Realizing that they could slip past the Errorunsai's armies, the Verdarites would move down to the Ifloract's home. The Depths of Flame would be besieged, and the Edhrine would win the war with the Ifloract before it even started.

Verdar VI looked around. The enemies were inside the mountain, surrounded and unable to escape. Verdar VI, however, knew from experience that they seemed to have infinite food and did not require rest. That meant a long siege would do nothing. Verdar VI could wait for more catapults, but he had other ideas. The enemy was not defending the roads that went out of the South Morhor Mountains. Verdar VI could return to his homelands, he could go to the Centaur Woods, he could go to the Eastern Desert, or he could go to the Elemental Mountains. Verdar VI decided he would attack the Depths of Flame.

The Ifloract was furious once he realized the Edhrine's trap. In anger, the Ifloract had demanded the Edhrine reissue his order. The Edhrine tricked him into leaving his base vulnerable. When the Ifloract went to the Edhrine and mocked him for allowing this, the Edhrine simply stated that that was his intention. The Ifloract needed to do something fast.

16

The Conquest

Verdar VI looked on as his armies marched out of the South Morhor Mountains. He glanced back and saw the Ifloract's Army moving desperately to defend its home. Where were the spiders and the dark spearmen? Verdar VI did not care. None of them would be able to reach the Depths of Flame in time. Verdar VI would not be able to flood it, since his wagons of water were destroyed, but he'd simply storm it.

The Edhrine watched as the Ifloract's Army marched southward. The Edhrine knew that he was too late. The Verdarites were going to get into the Depths of Flame. Without the legions of ashen soldiers to guard the door, the Verdarites will be able to walk in. They would not conquer the place, but they would cause damage.

"Mokror, we should go toward the Verdarite homeland now," the Edhrine announced.

The Mokror replied, "I will get my spiders moving."

With that, the Edhrine advanced his own troops on the march towards the North Morhor Plain. That was the next Verdarite territory. The Edhrine and the Mokror were no longer on the defensive. They were attacking the Verdarites.

"Do you know the location of the Verdarite capital?" the Edhrine asked.

The Mokror answered, "No, but we think it's in the North Morhor Plain, where we are going. That was the first place they conquered, and every other location was free at the time."

"What about the Dead Mountains?" the Edhrine continued with his questioning.

The Mokror answered again, "Who would be crazy enough to base up in those barren mountains. They are not very defensible, since they have gentle slopes. That is, until a certain point, where it becomes an impossible cliff. Those mountains are like a wall."

"Alright, then," the Edhrine said.

The Edhrine and the Mokror arrived at the North Morhor Plains at night. By then, he could see the Ifloract's armies speed marching. They were about a mile behind the Edhrine.

"Wait for the Ifloract to catch up to us," the Edhrine directed.

When the Ifloract caught up, he barely kept himself from lunging at the Edhrine.

"I have to use a great effort to keep myself from killing you," the Ifloract declared.

"No matter. We need to get the help of the Marantaur," the Edhrine stated.

"What?" the Mokror questioned.

"I know that you and he had a...disagreement that may have resulted in a few dead spiders and tribesmen, but he lives here and can probably help us," the Edhrine explained.

"Fine, then, but I do not want to fight beside that idiot of a beast for long," the Mokror complained.

"Of course. Remember, we already have one war that will be

occurring after the Verdarites fall, between the Ifloract and I. You can make a similar arrangement with the Marantaur," the Edhrine suggested.

"Oh, I probably will," the Mokror promised.

"With that settled, I want to kill some Verdarites. There's a village over there, most likely captured by the Verdarites," the Ifloract said, facing towards a nearby village. They could all see the Verdarite banner flying from a small tower in the center.

"Surround it and use spiders to scale the wall. I think two spiders could lift one of my spearmen. Send them over the wall and ambush our enemies," the Edhrine said.

A Verdarite commander stood in the center of the village. He had been running it smoothly, posting guards, and directing the villagers. They were now prisoners of the Verdarite Empire, and they would work the fields until they died fueling the Verdarite war machine. The commander would be promoted if he could increase the size of his fields. That's what he forced the villagers to work on. The commander looked at the group of huts the villagers were demolishing. Those huts were in the way. The commander was about to walk over when he heard the sound of metal on wood. The commander turned to the village wall and saw strange dark spearmen and large spiders rushing towards him. The commander frantically pulled out a dagger to defend himself but took a spear to the stomach before he could use it.

The Edhrine looked from the top of the village wall into the village. The Verdarites had villagers as prisoners, and they forced them to work the fields. The Verdarite commander was dead on the ground, and many other Verdarites were as well. The Edhrine ordered spiders to climb into the village tower and eliminate any Verdarites hiding within. The tower, the Edhrine guessed, was an original structure in the village that the villagers would hide in during an attack. The Edhrine turned his attention to the other living Verdarites. He put his sword in its sheath and lunged at a Verdarite spearman from the side. The Edhrine stole a dagger from the Verdarite's belt and thrust it into the spearman's neck. Moving on, the Edhrine took out his sword and killed another Verdarite. Dodging an arrow, the Edhrine destroyed another spearman with a thrust to the abdomen and then turned around and threw his sword at an archer. The Edhrine calmly walked over and retrieved his sword, surrounded by the fallen Verdarite division.

"Edhrine, the village is clear," the Edhrine's first soldier reported.

"Excellent. Prepare to march on the next village," the Edhrine directed.

Two months later, the entire North Morhor Plains was liberated of Verdarite control. With the help of the Marantaur, who they found wandering the plains, the villages had been attacked and freed.

The six legions that attacked the Errorunsai in the South Morhor Mountains were conquering the Eastern Desert. The Eastern Desert had barely anything worthwhile within it, and the Edhrine was not about to defend that wasteland. The only resistance the Verdarites encountered was by nomads, and the nomads probably wouldn't care about a Verdarite occupation. That was, unless the Verdarites attacked first. The Edhrine reasoned that the nomads could outrun the Verdarites since they were on horses and wagons.

"Where is their capital?" the Edhrine asked.

"Not in the North Morhor Plains," the Mokror replied.

"It must be somewhere in the Dead Mountains, then. It can't

be in the Centaur Woods because we would have heard about it. It can't be in the South Morhor Mountains because we attacked that area, and we would know about any capitals there. It can't be in the North Morhor Plain because we searched the entire place. It can't be anywhere else because the first attack was on the North Morhor Plain and their capital must be adjacent to it," the Edhrine reasoned.

"Seems correct to me. I will send spiders to scout the mountains," the Mokror said.

A week later, the spiders reported that there was nothing on the Dead Mountains themselves, but they found what appeared to be a ravine pass, with eerie statues of the Edhrine's militia attacking Sentinels.

"Why are there statues of my fallen militia men fighting Sentinels? Why are there statues at all?" the Edhrine wondered aloud.

"Let's conquer the capital and ask the Verdarites," the Ifloract offered.

The Edhrine got his soldiers on the march, and they reached the ravine pass within the day. They quickly discovered that the ravine pass was more like a maze. The Mokror's spiders, however, managed to find the way through. The Edhrine, with his dark spearmen, marched at the front in an arrowhead formation. Behind him, the Ifloract's living flames and ashen soldiers marched in a phalanx, the former floating above. Behind those, the Mokror and her spiders marched. Behind her, the Marantaur, a massive beast with two great maces went forward himself.

They also discovered that something was very wrong with the empty plain beyond the ravine. The Edhrine heard his soldiers murmuring something about a mutiny.

"What are you talking about?" the Edhrine demanded.

Instantly, two of the Edhrine's spearmen attacked him. The Edhrine dispatched them with his sword and looked around. All the other spearmen marched normally. The Edhrine looked back at the others. He saw the Mokror standing over a dead spider and the Ifloract looking confused at a dead ashen soldier. The Edhrine motioned for them to come to him.

"Why did my soldiers attack me?" the Ifloract asked.

"This place explains everything. Dark sorcery is strong enough to possess. If we are to succeed, we press forward alone. Send the armies to the North Morhor Plain, and leave someone behind to command them. The rest of us shall press forth through this barren plain and find their capital," the Edhrine explained.

"Alright. Ifloract, you stay outside. The Edhrine, the Marantaur, and I will go in," the Mokror said.

The Ifloract floated back towards the ravine maze without a word and the other three Errorunsai continued without their armies.

After a few hours of walking, the Errorunsai spotted something in the distance. It resembled a fortress of the Southlands, but much larger. They continued on wordlessly. When they got closer, they found many tents, but no soldiers within them.

"This must be where the six legions live when they are not on the march," the Edhrine observed.

He received no response from the other two Errorunsai with him. They continued walking through the empty camps. The ground in that dark plain was stone, like the mountains, and the air was a dead gray. No evidence of life, save for the Verdarites, could be found in the plain.

"I wonder if anyone is home," the Mokror said, eyeing the

fortress.

Then, they spotted a guard on the wall. They all ducked behind something, except the massive Marantaur, who stayed still hoping they wouldn't notice him.

"There's no way the Marantaur could do a stealthy infiltration. He has to stay behind this rock if we're going to assassinate the emperor," the Mokror noted.

"She's right," the Edhrine said, looking at the Marantaur, "Stay here. I'll signal you if we need you to charge in and help us out."

The Edhrine and the Mokror stealthily made their way to the fortress and looked around.

"Looks like there's only two gates, on opposite sides," the Mokror said.

"They're both guarded. We're going over the wall," the Edhrine declared.

"We don't have spiders. How do we scale it?" the Mokror asked.

The Edhrine responded, "That tent looks like it stores weapons. Let's see if anyone left their swords behind.

A few minutes later, the Edhrine walked out of the tent with a sack full of swords. He began thrusting the swords into the wall, into the seams between bricks. The sword blades stayed in the wall quite well.

"Let's move," the Edhrine announced.

The Edhrine and the Mokror used the sword hilts as handholds to climb up the wall. Seeing no guards in the immediate vicinity at the top, they looked towards the center of the fortress. Instead of a wall surrounding a courtyard with a keep in the middle, the wall was part of the keep. That meant there would be a door on the wall that would go inside the fortress, where the Edhrine wanted to be.

"Over here," the Mokror whispered.

The Edhrine went over and climbed down the hatch the Mokror found. Moving stealthily, the Edhrine and the Mokror found a small room, which appeared to be a lounge. In the middle was a table surrounded by chairs. The Edhrine and the Mokror sat down across from each other and started thinking over plans. They were trying to eliminate the Verdarite emperor, with the goal of bringing the entire Verdarite Empire down with him. The emperor's throne room would most likely be either in the very top or the very bottom of the keep, since that was the location of most thrones.

"Let's go downstairs and look there first. I have a feeling he will be there," the Mokror said.

The Edhrine agreed, and they made their way through several hallways and staircases towards the bottom of the fort. After several near-encounters with Verdarite guards, the Mokror and the Edhrine were right behind the front gate of the fortress. They encountered a suspiciously large door. The Edhrine worked on slicing the lock, while the Mokror kept watch. After a few tries, the Edhrine destroyed the lock. They went through and closed the door again, making it seem like nothing had happened.

"This place reminds me of home," the Mokror said, observing the mossy bricks of the corridor.

The Edhrine replied, "This place indeed reminds me of your sewers. The corridor goes only one way: down. The emperor is bound to be down there."

The two Errorunsai continued moving down the corridor, carefully watching for traps and guards. Soon enough, they were in a big chamber at the bottom of the fortress. The cavernous room contained a large rocky throne in the rear.

Stalagmites and stalactites protruded from the floor and ceiling of the massive cave. An eerie gray mist filled the entire room, lowering visibility.

"This is definitely the place," the Mokror declared.

"Indeed, it is," the Edhrine agreed.

Seeing no use for stealth anymore, the two Errorunsai walked calmly towards the throne, weapons out. They continued forward, unable to see who was on the throne through the mist. Once close enough, they saw the throne was empty.

"What!" a surprised Mokror exclaimed.

"He is not here. We must wait," the Edhrine said.

They heard a loud, repetitive thumping noise. "The legions are returning. They will see our daggers in the wall," the Edhrine said.

"We need to get the Marantaur out of there. Where is he going to hide?" the Mokror asked. "We should have never brought him along."

"Remind me why you care if the Marantaur is killed," the Edhrine calmly asked.

The Mokror replied, "You know, that's a good point. The guards will assume he placed the daggers, and I have enough issues with him. Let's wait behind the throne. When the emperor comes, we will take him together."

Outside, the Marantaur hid inside a large tent. He was way too big for this, but he had to make do. Hoping that no Verdarites came to the tent, the Marantaur crouched down, holding a Verdarite spear in his hand. There was not enough room to swing a mace inside the tent, so the Verdarite spear would have to do if anyone came in.

Back in the throne room, the Edhrine heard footsteps entering the throne room. He counted eight people in the room.

"Have the legions go to their tents. I will take some time to strategize before our next attack," a voice said.

"Yes, my emperor," another voice responded.

The Mokror eyed the Edhrine. He nodded. The Edhrine heard footsteps leaving. He counted three. Three people left the room, leaving five there.

"Sir, there were daggers on the wall. Infiltrators may be in the fort," said a different voice.

"Make sure everything is locked down," the emperor instructed.

The Edhrine heard footsteps near the throne. He nodded again to the Mokror. The Edhrine signaled to the Mokror with his hand. Three. Two. One. The Edhrine and the Mokror charged out and engaged the emperor's bodyguards. The bodyguards were skilled, but the Edhrine was more skilled. Stealing a dagger from one bodyguard's sheath, the Edhrine threw it into a bodyguard. One down, three to go. The Mokror sliced one bodyguard in half using her sword-like weapon. The weapon was a sword with an axe on the end blade and a spike at the bottom of the hilt. The weapon was deadly, and it was proving its value in parrying enemy blows as well. The Edhrine then got another kill, decapitating a guard from behind. The Edhrine and the Mokror turned towards the last guard.

"You shall never defeat Verdar. My emperor shall reign!" the last guard shouted.

Rushing at the Edhrine, the guard thrusted his spear forward. The Edhrine dodged the guard's rush and allowed the Mokror to plant her axe blade in his back. The Edhrine finished the guard with his sword.

"At last," said the emperor on the throne. The Edhrine and the Mokror turned to face him, weapons at the ready.

"Your weapons will not save you from my power," the emperor declared.

"Your armies will not save you from the Errorunsai," the Mokror replied.

"And so, you shall fall!" the emperor bellowed, using sorcery to shove both the Edhrine and the Mokror backwards.

They regained their footing and rushed at the emperor, only to be shoved back again via sorcery. The Edhrine decided that it was time to use his own sorcery. Grabbing a loose pebble from the ground, the Edhrine used sorcery to fling it at the Verdarite emperor. The pebble hit the emperor's arm at high velocity. The emperor did not seem to be affected, but the blood on his arm suggested otherwise.

"The Verdarites shall defeat you!" the emperor shouted.

The Edhrine was done talking. He rushed the emperor again, but this time used sorcery to launch his sword at the wounded emperor. The sword hit the emperor square in the chest, but the emperor did not go down.

"Pain has no power over me!" the emperor screamed, now acting more and more insane.

The Edhrine realized he needed a weapon. Grabbing more loose pebbles, he barraged the emperor, which gave the Mokror an opening to get behind him. The Mokror slashed downwards with her weapon, decapitating the emperor and killing him once and for all. The Edhrine retrieved his sword and observed the fallen emperor.

"We need to get out of here," the Edhrine said.

"Which way?" the Mokror asked, eyeing the corridor, "They probably heard the emperor's insane screaming. They're going to be coming."

"This throne room doesn't have other exits," the Edhrine said.

The Edhrine felt strange. Even though the emperor was dead, the Edhrine felt a dark presence lurking about in the throne room. Earlier he assumed the darkness he felt was the emperor, but the emperor was dead. Either way, the Edhrine had to leave.

"Edhrine, there's a waterfall on this end of the cave. The water looks…foul, but we can probably get out that way," the Mokror observed.

"Let's get out of here," the Edhrine remarked.

They climbed to the top of the waterfall using the rocks to the side of it and crawled out into a small reservoir of water. They were still in the fortress. It appeared that the reservoir was simply water storage, as it was right next to what appeared to be the mess hall. It also apparently functioned as a decoration for the throne room.

Back outside the fortress, the Marantaur heard footsteps coming towards his tent. He readied the Verdarite spear he had. When a Verdarite soldier who had only a shield came through the door, he was surprised to get speared hard enough to send him flying out of the tent. The Marantaur chuckled to himself, and then realized that the entire camp was likely staring at the dead body outside the tent. The Marantaur grabbed his maces and got ready to rip up the tent once the Verdarites came.

The Edhrine and the Mokror snuck through the mess hall and some hallways, while guards rushed towards the throne room. The Edhrine and the Mokror soon got past the wave of guards rushing to the throne room and had a clear path to the wall. They left the way they came in, climbing down the sword hilts sticking out of the wall. They stopped in their tracks and stared into the camp, spotting a catapult being moved towards a large tent.

"The Marantaur is in danger," the Edhrine emotionlessly

stated.

The Mokror responded, "I don't know why I want to help him, but I do. We need to distract them."

"There. There is another catapult. Do you see the torch over there? We can burn the other catapult to distract them," the Edhrine said.

The Marantaur waited, but no other Verdarites came into his tent. He wasn't sure why they hadn't yet. They knew he killed someone. Why weren't they coming in to kill him? The only thing the Marantaur heard outside was the noises of soldiers marching around and the sound of catapults rolling around. He wasn't quite sure why catapults were moving, but he didn't care. He just needed the next Verdarite to come in and get smashed.

The Edhrine put the torch to the catapult. He looked around. Nobody noticed. The Edhrine decided to fire the catapult to make sure it grabbed their attention. The Edhrine pulled the lever and ran into a nearby tent. He heard the sound of confused guards. Now, the Mokror needed to do her part.

The Mokror walked towards the catapult that was aimed at the large tent. No doubt the Marantaur was in there, oblivious to the fact that a catapult was about to crush him. Taking a torch, the Mokror lit the catapult and fled the scene.

The Marantaur now heard the sounds of fire. He shredded the tent around him with his maces and the horns on his helmet. Looking around, he saw legions of Verdarites encamped around the fortress, and a flaming catapult aiming at him. The Marantaur went into a rage and began smashing Verdarites with his maces, taking more arrows from them than he could count. The Marantaur was unaffected by the arrows, protected by his thick hide. The Verdarites were the ones running.

The Edhrine heard the Marantaur raging. He jumped out of

the tent and ran towards the chaos, hoping the Marantaur was being smart for once.

The Mokror sliced one Verdarite and then another, staying clear of the Marantaur's charge. She saw the Edhrine running towards her, looking for Verdarites.

"We need to find the the Ifloract. The Verdarites must have broken through his defenses. We sent the Ifloract to guard the pass. That is the only way to the fort." the Edhrine declared.

"Marantaur, we're leaving!" the Mokror announced.

The Marantaur was making too much noise to hear her, though. He was bashing through tents and crushing catapults with his maces.

"MARANTAUR, WE ARE LEAVING!" the Edhrine yelled.

The Marantaur looked over and came to the Edhrine. He was covered in arrows, but he seemed fine.

"What did you say?" the Marantaur asked.

"We are leaving," the Mokror answered.

With that, the three Errorunsai sprinted away from the fortress, pursued by the legions of Verdarites.

Outside the ravine pass, the Ifloract was searching a village. He had seen the Verdarite legions approaching, and they had turned towards that village. He did not know how the Verdarites had disappeared, but they did. The legions entered the village and then disappeared. The Ifloract entered the last hut, and found a trapdoor. Opening it, he found an underground tunnel big enough for a massive phalanx to march through. It led towards the ravine pass the Ifloract was guarding. The Ifloract rushed out of the house and ordered his army to start moving towards the ravine.

The Edhrine looked back at the charging legions and continued running forward. The Marantaur took a large rock and threw it backwards, killing some of the Verdarite spearmen.

"It's about time these Verdarites figured out their leader is dead!" the Mokror shouted as she threw a dagger backwards.

"DIE!" the Marantaur screamed, throwing another rock backwards at the Verdarites.

They all kept running, hoping the Ifloract was still guarding the ravine pass.

At the ravine pass, the Ifloract rushed with the Errorunsai's armies towards the Verdarites. He had to get to the fortress and warn the other Errorunsai about the legions. Still, he couldn't bring the armies. The dark sorcery would possess them. He had to go alone.

"Stay here and guard this pass with your lives," the Ifloract ordered the soldiers. He floated into the ravine maze.

Eventually, the four Errorunsai ran into each other. The Ifloract was confused as to why the legions were leaving the fort and chasing the others, but the three Errorunsai told him they would explain why later. The four Errorunsai soon reached the ravine maze, and, followed closely by the legions, reached the pass.

"Where are my spearmen?" the Edhrine asked, looking at the Ifloract.

"They are on the front lines, facing outwards. Now, that has become the rear since the Verdarites are behind us," the Ifloract corrected.

"The Verdarites are catching up!" the Mokror yelled.

The Ifloract ordered the nearest ashen soldiers to point their long halberds at the Verdarites. They did, and a few Verdarites were unable to stop running in time to avoid being impaled. The Errorunsai were safely behind the wall of halberds, facing the Verdarites.

"I want my archers up here," the Edhrine told a group of nearby spearmen.

"As you command," the spearman replied. The spearman went to the rear ranks to get the Edhrine's archers.

"What must we do?" asked the archer closest to the Edhrine.

"Open fire," the Edhrine commanded.

The Edhrine's archers struck a few of the Verdarite spearmen, but the Verdarites put up their shields, barring any arrows from getting into their phalanx.

"Hold your fire," the Edhrine directed.

The Verdarites kept their shields up.

"Spearmen, move in front of the Ifloract's soldiers," the Edhrine instructed.

The Ifloract's halberds were long, but the ashen soldiers carrying them did not have shields because both hands were required to hold the twenty-foot-long halberd. The Edhrine's spearmen positioned themselves in front of the ashen soldiers, forming a wall with their shields. The ashen soldiers extended their long halberds over the shield wall. They now had a shield in front of them without losing the length advantage of the halberds.

"Charge!" the Edhrine ordered. The Verdarite shield wall was holding up, but it would eventually break from the assault of the halberdiers.

The Edhrine watched and waited until the first Verdarite soldier was killed. One of the Ifloract's pikemen managed to force his pike through the Verdarite shield wall and killed the soldier. That left a small gap in the shield wall, but one big enough for the Edhrine's next move. He ordered a few of his soldiers to part, allowing him through. The Edhrine charged towards the enemy shield wall. As expected, someone from the second line came to take his fallen comrade's position, but the Edhrine was too fast for the Verdarite reaction. He used his sword to parry the Verdarite spears and ran into the middle of their formation. A swordsman always had an advantage over polearms, and the Edhrine wasn't just any swordsman. The Verdarites would have quite a difficult time. The Edhrine chewed through the tight Verdarite formation from within, carving a path of destruction. The Verdarites had difficulty fighting back with such little room to maneuver and only spears and shields. However, the Edhrine still had a long way to go if he was to defeat the Verdarites. It was time for his next move.

"Attack!" the Edhrine shouted.

The spearmen and the ashen pikemen charged forward, while the Edhrine targeted the front line. Unable to fight both the Edhrine's troops and the Edhrine himself, the Verdarites were defeated even more quickly in the front. With the front line being crushed, the next rows of Verdarite soldiers advanced to take their place. However, the Edhrine repeated the obliteration. Suddenly, however, the Edhrine heard a noise. He recognized it all too well.

"Catapults! Retreat!" the Edhrine yelled.

The Edhrine himself ran back from the rain of stones and looked with satisfaction as the Verdarites troops, who gave chase to the Edhrine, were crushed by their own catapults.

"Attack!" the Edhrine shouted again, this time keeping his eyes out for the Verdarite catapults.

The Edhrine heard the sound again. This time, he noticed where the stones came from. The catapults were outside the ravine maze, and out of view. The Edhrine ordered everyone to retreat again to avoid the stones crushing them. The Verdarites learned from the last time and did not give chase. After that next barrage, the Edhrine almost ordered his troops to charge again before realizing that the Verdarite catapults were now firing at will, keeping the Edhrine's army from advancing.

The dust from the stones' impact obscured vision for both sides. The Edhrine used this cloud to his advantage. He ordered his spearmen to give him their daggers, which they wouldn't need unless they lost their spears. The Edhrine shoved the daggers into various crevices in the ravine wall, testing them to make sure they were strong handholds. They were since they were constructed of Edhormond steel and the strange yellow mist. The Edhrine began climbing, adding daggers ahead of him as he went. Soon, he was high enough to see over the cloud of dust. The Verdarites were simply standing and waiting. The Edhrine used the daggers to go sideways. When he was directly over the Verdarite army, the Edhrine descended. He placed dagger after dagger into the wall of the ravine maze, continuing down to the Verdarite army.

Once the Edhrine was low enough to safely jump down into the horde of Verdarites, he jumped. Pointing his sword down during the fall, the Edhrine killed the first Verdarite with his landing. He began slashing with his sword outward, parrying the Verdarite spears and destroying the phalanx. When the Verdarites noticed, the catapults stopped firing. This was the Edhrine's opportunity.

"Forward!" the Edhrine shouted.

His troops charged and engaged the phalanx. The Verdarites lost men as they had before. This time, however, the Edhrine's army pushed forward, without giving the next line of Verdarites a chance to advance. The Edhrine and his army were winning, shredding through the Verdarites.

The Ifloract floated above the army with his living flames,

barraging the Verdarites. Between the Edhrine, the Ifloract, and their armies, the Verdarites were losing. The Edhrine called for his archers to fire. The Verdarites had to simultaneously defend against the Edhrine slashing through their ranks, the army charging at them, the Ifloract and his living flames barraging them, and now the archers firing at them. The Verdarites were beyond overwhelmed.

The Edhrine and his men continued to destroy the Verdarites, when unexpectedly the legions stopped fighting. They began marching in different directions, seemingly conflicted. Without warning, they began fighting each other. The Edhrine looked around, and finally spotted the small hill from which the Verdarite commanders led their army. He could see fire and fighting. The Verdarites had realized the emperor was dead and their leaders were trying to become the next emperor. The Verdarite armies fought their way towards the commanders, killing each other randomly. The Edhrine watched the once-organized Verdarite host descend into chaos. The Edhrine was almost positive that the legions killed their own commanders and were now fighting to the last man. The Verdarites killed each other for hours, until at last only one stood, surrounded by his fallen comrades. The Edhrine approached, sword out. The Verdarite died celebrating.

The Edhrine heard fire behind him. He knew exactly what it was. Rolling to the side, the Edhrine dodged the Ifloract's first barrage. The war had begun, as promised. The Edhrine saw the Marantaur fighting the Mokror and her spiders, too. The Verdarites were done infighting. Now, it was the Errorunsai's turn.

The Edhrine lunged at the Ifloract, but the Ifloract materialized his obsidian sword and blocked the strike. The Edhrine and the Ifloract dueled, both making use of sorcery to attempt to gain an advantage. The Edhrine moved towards the ravine maze, and the Ifloract followed him. The two swords clashed the entire way. Neither of them said anything. Upon reaching the ravine maze, the Edhrine and the Ifloract's respective armies joined them. The duel became a battle of armies. The Edhrine and the Ifloract ended up in the back lines of their own armies, far from each other.

"Charge, and use your spears to parry the Ifloract's pikes. Keep your shields up to avoid the living flames' salvo," the Edhrine directed his spearmen.

The Ifloract's pikemen were losing, and the Edhrine was winning. The Edhrine hoped that the entire war would continue in same way.

Glossary

Dark Mountains: Mountains made impregnable by ancient sorcery. The sorcery was the primary reason that the Verdarites decided to move to the Dead Plain, which was surrounded by the Dark Mountains.

Dead Maze: A maze of meandering, narrow ravines within the Dead Mountains that led to the Dead Plain.

Dead Plain: A plain filled with evil sorcery, home of the Verdarite Empire. It was surrounded by the impenetrable Dark Mountains.

Depths of Flame: Home of the Ifloract and his army, situated in the Mountains of the Elements.

Edhormond: Stone soldiers based from Edhormon; of or relating to Edhormon.

Edhormond Mountains: A range of mountains that were known for having nothing of value in them. This soon changed, however, when the Edhrine created the Edhormond army.

Edhormond Steel: A strong, black steel used by the Edhrine's later army that formed in a type of rare crystal.

Edhrine: The Errorunsin who was the leader of the stone Edhormond soldiers. He started with an army of humans, but when the Verdarite Empire destroyed that army, he began to rely on the sorcery-driven stone soldiers.

Edhrine's Militia: The army of humans lead by the Edhrine. This army was primarily focused on keeping its own members alive and fighting the Sentinels.

Errorunsai: Four long-living, powerful beings who were excellent duelists and powerful sorcerers.

Errorunsin: The singular form of Errorunsai.

Ifloract: The Errorunsin who led an army of ashen soldiers and living flames and lives in the Depth of Flames.

Ifloract's Army: Ashen soldiers and living flames created by the Ifloract.

Marantaur: A great beast of an Errorunsin, known for his great size and strength but rather low intelligence.

Mohraight: A nation in the southlands based around the river of the same name; the capital city of the nation of the same name. The city was a frequent stop of the Edhrine when he needed his ships repaired or modified.

Mohraight Graveyard: A huge area of rocks located southeast of the Edhormond Mountains filled with rotting bodies and ships that surrounds the home of the Mokror.

Mokror: The Errorunsin who led legions of spiders and lived on an island in the center of the Mohraight Graveyard.

Mokror's Spiders: The giant spiders and other creations created by the Mokror.

Nations of the Southlands: A collection of nations south of Edhormon that was comprised of Mohraight Kingdom, Nacreato, Monfor, Laste, Traste, Acronomon, Lacon, Zser, Zygyptania, and Ysio.

North Morhor Plain: A plain that was known for having many villages and tribes almost constantly at war. It was also the home of the Marantaur.

Sentinels: A nation of soldiers that had forts scattered around the world. They usually did not inhabit all forts at once, moving from location to location as needed. They were the enemy of the Edhrine.

South Morhor Mountains: A mountain range situated beneath the North Morhor Plain.

Sorwond: A city that was on the western shore of the Mohraight River. It was a frequent stop for traders.

Verdarite Empire: An empire that eventually found its way to the Dead Plain. There, it was corrupted by sorcery and turned into the evil, bloodthirsty empire that attempted to conquer the world.

Also by Braden Quinlan

THE ERRORUNSAI
In the tyrannical kingdom of Sorwond, a king ruled over his people with an iron fist, manipulating them with sorcery to do his will. One boy named Joseph escaped the kingdom and formed a rebellion and liberated Sorwond. However, a larger evil was on the horizon. Little did Joseph know, he would play one of the largest roles in fighting it. Embark with Joseph on a series of adventures as the Prophecy of the Errorunsai is realized.

www.ingramcontent.com/pod-product-compliance
Lightning Source LLC
Chambersburg PA
CBHW030814200726
48288CB00004B/1236